SWORDS OF FIRE

Edited by
G. W. Thomas

RAGE m a c h i n e Books
Canada

First Edition
First Trade Paperback Printing January 2010

Cover art, design and interior illustrations: M. D. Jackson

Editor's Note

Each story in this anthology is a work of fiction. Names, places, characters, and incidents in this anthology are either the product of the author's imagination or used fictitiously. Any resemblance to real people (living or dead) places, business establishments, locales, and/or events is entirely coincidental.

CONTENTS

Introduction

I DON'T think anyone would disagree that the late 1960s and early 1970s were the heydays of Sword & Sorcery. Starting with the Lancer reprints of Conan as well as important anthologies like *The Fantastic Swordsmen* (1967, L. Sprague de Camp) and *The Mighty Barbarians* (1969, Hans Stefan Santesson), fans quickly discovered the excitement of Hyborian tales from writers like Robert E. Howard, Fritz Leiber, Poul Anderson and Lin Carter. This same time period saw important new writers like John Jakes, Roger Zelazny, Avram Davidson, Jack Vance in the pages of *Fantastic Stories*, the most important S&S mag after *Weird Tales*. Anti-S&S was also adding new directions in the pages of *Fantasy & Science Fiction* with stories by Larry Niven and George Alec Effinger. In 1970, *Conan the Barbarian* exploded onto the comic scene, scripted by Roy Thomas and artwork of Barry Smith. For the next decade everything that wasn't Tolkienian Fantasy, was Sword & Sorcery.

One of the highlights for 1973 was the publishing of two

paperback anthologies (one book really, divided into two), called *Flashing Swords*. Unlike the anthologies that came before, *Flashing Swords* #1 and #2 published all-new tales of a longer length, novellas of 15,000 words, too long for most magazines. The first volume featured a Fafhrd & Grey Mouser tale by Fritz Leiber, a Dying Earth tale by Jack Vance, a Viking era saga by Poul Anderson and a comedic piece by Lin Carter. The second volume had a Pusadian tale from L. Sprague de Camp, an Elric epic by Michael Moorcock, a Witch World piece by Andre Norton and a Brak story from John Jakes. And to top it all off, two covers from the brush of the master, Frank Frazetta.

I miss the days of 1973. I was 10 years old and was just discovering Sword & Sorcery through comic books. The first S&S comic I bought was *Creatures on the Loose* #23 (May 1973) that featured the second half of the "Thieves of Zangabal" adaptation based on Lin Carter's Thongor story. As I grew older, became a confident reader, Sword & Sorcery was a large part of my reading menu. I discovered Solomon Kane first, then Conan, Thongor, King Kull, Bran Mak Morn and Brak of the yellow braid. It was an exciting time to be a fan.

The 1980s rang in changes. The film version of *Conan the Barbarian* (1982) and many bad imitations brought a new disdain for Sword & Sorcery. Along with this was the blending of S&S with Tolkienian Fantasy, largely through the auspices of Fantasy role-playing games like *Advanced Dungeons & Dragons*™. Fantasy publishing moved onto bigger and bigger bestsellers but shied away from identifiable Sword & Sorcery. By the 1990s the only books that could be instantly recognized as S&S were Conan pastiches and role-playing game books like *Forgotten Realms*.

But the pendulum always swings back. With the works of Robert E. Howard entering the public domain, the stories that started it all back in *Weird Tales* in the 1930s, then fueled the renaissance of the 1960s in reprints, are now available online, and free to anyone. This availability has brought renewed interest in all things S&S. And it seems a good time to reintroduce the *Flashing Swords* style anthology. Here it is—

Swords of Fire. Four novella-length stories—too long for most magazines even today, perhaps in our days of flash fiction attention spans, even more so—not reprints but new stories by new writers, those cranky babies who cut their teeth on four-color barbarians back in the 1970s, all grown up and writing new tales of swordsmen and women, sorcerers, magic and dark realms. *Hail!* fellow traveler, as we embark into lands of flashing swords and midnight suns. ❋

- G. W. Thomas

Temple Of The Rakshasa

David A. Hardy

Robert E. Howard drew much of his inspiration for 'Sword & Sorcery' from the historical adventure fiction of the 1920s, found in magazines like Adventure. *(S&S was a label Howard never used—it was coined by Fritz Leiber in the 1940s.) These tales by Harold Lamb, Talbot Mundy, E. Hoffman Price, Achmed Abdullah and others were set in authentic locales like India, Syria, Iran or during the Crusades. Howard's own prehistoric era, the Hyborian Age, resembles proto-history, an age forgotten, allowing him to add a supernatural element that the likes of Lamb would never have done. Working in this tradition today, David A. Hardy has this same of love of history, color, pageantry and monsters, perhaps even more so than Howard did. I can think of no author who does it better than this Texan (not David A. Hardy who is the English SF artist). Hardy takes us into the world of post-Alexandrian India for this tale of gods and warriors.*

THE JUNGLE was still, no breath of wind moved, no bird shrilled, nor did the children of Hanuman chatter and romp in the branches above. Godarz the Tokhari sat on his horse, listening for sounds that did not come. There was only his horse's breath and the beating of his heart. He drew his bow from its case and fitted an arrow to the string. What Godarz heard was the sound of an ambush.

Sweat ran in streams down his face and dripped down his red beard. Under his iron scale armor his jacket and trousers were soaked. His helmet felt like a cooking pot. Godarz swore, by Buddha and by Zeus and by gods whose names have been forgotten, that should he live one thousand years he would never get used to the heat in India. Yet despite the heat his eyes glittered like cold jade. He remembered well the warning of the sage Vasudeva, "The path to the Kali-vraisya treasure is washed in the blood of those who seek it!"

Godarz was a son of the high steppe, born in a felt tent and reared on a horse. His people were nomadic herdsman and warriors. Feuds and wars had driven them west. In the colonies founded by mighty Alexander along the Hindu Kush Godarz found employment as a mercenary, hiring his sword to the Greek kinglets and Indian rajahs in their interminable wars.

For a fleeting moment he thought he heard a voice, pitched low, but with a musical lilt. He laid down the reins of his steed over a branch. Godarz advanced cautiously through the jungle creepers, bow and arrow ready. He pressed into a small clearing and then swore bitterly.

Three women were there, dressed alike in Skythian jackets, Indian kilts and Greek corselets. Swords were on their hips and their bows were at the ready. Godarz knew them: Tomyris, Parysatis, and Roxane, the war-sisters.

They were of the Saka tribe, whose girls learned to ride and shoot as well as men. They too had drifted south, taking the mercenary trail like Godarz. Greek kings and native rajahs eagerly paid for Amazons to decorate their palaces. Godarz had learned they were anything but mere decoration.

He had met them in Ghandhara where traders, mercenaries, sophists, and saddhus brawled, caroused, and preached below the Khyber Pass. In the capital of King Menander, for the man with gold in his purse there was wine, song and above all, women. There were dancing girls from the Tamil lands, with dainty feet that spurned the earth, bold-eyed Phrygians, passionate in love but far too handy with knives, and buxom Greek lasses, who dallied most willingly as long as their bull-necked and belligerent brothers weren't about. But to Godarz they were pale sparks compared to the burning flame of Roxane. Her ice-blue eyes and raven hair haunted his thoughts.

Roxane and Godarz reveled through soft Punjabi nights. No man had roused Roxane's passion so well as the wolfish nomad. And none had loathed Godarz so well as Tomyris. The Sakas had ancient feuds with the Tokhari, and Tomyris hated Godarz.

Then came the day when the gold was gone and the passion spent. A league of rajahs had planned the doom of King Menander. The mercenary road called and Godarz parted from Roxane. When next he saw the war-sisters, it was across a battlefield. Their meeting was brief and unsatisfactory, but the fate of a strong castle was decided to great advantage to a Punjabi king.

"Lo, the Tokhari dog has sniffed the scent of gold," Parysatis sneered.

"Silence!" Tomyris said. "Chandra the dacoit is on our trail!"

Godarz and the women returned to a state of watchfulness, as much for each other as for any outside foe. Whatever their rivalries, they had no wish to be taken by Chandra's raiders. He was a formidable captain of bandits who ruled the jungle. Rumor had it that Chandra had selected this range because he too sought the Kali-vraisya temple and its fabled wealth.

Godarz scanned the tangled mass of green. A brief flash of

color, as of a patterned turban, was followed by movement. The Tokhari pointed. An arrow flew past his head and he shot back. Godarz shot quickly and heard a yelp of pain.

More arrows flew from the bush. One stuck in Godarz's armor. Howling curses, dacoits broke from the bush. Roxane shot one through the eye and then drew her sword to trade blows with an axe-wielding dacoit.

Godarz dropped his bow and whipped his sword out just in time to slash a dacoit who ran at him with a spear. As Godarz engaged the spearman, another dacoit tackled his legs and they collapsed together. The dacoit had the strength of a bull. He wrapped ape-like paws around Godarz's throat and throttled the Tokhari until his vision swam. Godarz vainly tried to break the dacoit's grip. With a last convulsive effort he smashed his helmeted head into the dacoit's face. The man released his hold and stumbled off in pain.

Godarz rose to his feet and took up his sword. Across the clearing Tomyris was furiously battling a dacoit, sword against sword. Roxane was still fending off her foe, but Parysatis was nowhere in sight. Godarz rushed forward to help the others when an arrow flew from above and transfixed Tomyris's foe between the shoulders. Godarz flung himself on Roxane's opponent. In a flash the dacoit was stretched dead in a pool of blood.

Parysatis dropped from a tree overhead. "Always take the high ground as old King Kosrav used to say. I got the one in the brush with the bow and the others ran off."

"May the divs and the rakshasas take them!" Godarz exclaimed. "Those dacoits will have stolen my horse!"

"Don't speak of the Ones who Dwell in Darkness." Roxane looked up at a vulture that had settled in a tree. The creature eyed the dead dacoits speculatively. "They can take many forms and be among us unknown. What kind of horse was it anyway?"

"It was a good stallion I got from King Menander's master of horse."

"I prefer a mare, myself," Tomyris said in a bored tone.

"Roxane rides a stallion but Parysatis will straddle either. Let's see your steed then." Tomyris pushed through the brush. The horse was still tethered to a tree by the trail. Tomyris loosed the reins and gave the animal a resounding slap.

"Divs take you woman!" Godarz swore as the horse bolted away. "What do you mean by that?"

"I mean we need none of you Tokhari!" Tomyris's voice was edged with steel.

"What, do you still resent that I had the better of you in that little war for Mathura castle? Or do you think you can find the temple treasure by yourselves? I tell you, you need me more than I need you!"

"Is that what you told Vasudeva before he died? How did he die? Where did the green residue that the temple servants found on his cup come from? We made the trip to Gandhara and asked. He was your friend Godarz! Maybe you could tell us?" Her hand strayed dangerously close to her sword.

"Aye, he was my friend! And the divs can gnaw your bones in Hell before I answer to you!" Warily Godarz moved up the trail after his horse. He listened for the sound of a bowstring, but none came and he moved more quickly.

As Godarz trudged on aching feet he cursed Tomyris and her war-sisters. But he also thought of Vasudeva. Godarz had met him in the temple district of Gandhara preaching on the Noble Eight-fold Path of the Buddha. At his side was an aristocratic Persian scholar named Artabanus. Vasudeva lectured on the peace that came with enlightenment and the illusion of the world and the soul. He illustrated his homilies with tales of the hero Rama, his bride Sita, and the Kali-vraisya Temple wherein Rama laid a great treasure and a greater curse.

"That treasure is a savage illusion," Vasudeva lectured. "He who is attached to greed will be crushed, sliced open, buried alive, slain, and re-born, yet all the gold in the Kali-vraisya crypt will not suffice to gain enlightenment."

"But there is a lot of gold, yes?" Godarz asked. He did not think that he was ready for enlightenment, but he could always use money. He had stayed to listen, not comprehending the message, but growing to love the messenger.

The time came when Godarz went away to war. He had met Roxane again, on the opposite side of a battlefield. When the war was over Godarz returned to Gandhara, but Vasudaeva was gone. His acolyte had vanished with Vasudeva's library. With neither teacher nor lover, Godarz had set out to find the Kali-vraisya temple.

Suddenly Godarz snapped from his reverie. He heard the snorting of horses and men speaking ahead. The men were talking in Greek. Godarz cursed again, for the second time this day he had encountered someone he knew and did not wish to meet. The Tokhari was about to step aside into the jungle when the speakers moved into view.

SIX MEN came riding down the trail, leading a pack donkey and Godarz's war-horse. They greeted Godarz like a lost brother.

"*Kaire*! Godarz, it is good to see you!" said the leader, a man with hawk-like eyes that darted back and forth between his beard and the Macedonian beret pulled low on his forehead.

"I wish I could say the same, Xeno."

"I brought Lykaeon. He says he doesn't hold a grudge over that time you knifed him."

"I've quite forgotten about how he shot an arrow in my leg from ambush and hired two Kali worshippers to strangle me. I don't know if they've gotten over it though. I killed them."

Lykaeon let out a low, animal snarl.

"I see you've come along too, Artabanush." Godarz nodded at Vasudeva's former acolyte. He was armed with a bow and sword like the others, but he was fleshy and soft where the others were hard and wolfish. He wore a massive silver ring that he stroked with appalling nervousness.

"Who are the others?" Godarz indicated three thuggish looking individuals.

"We hired them in Baktria. You are apt to meet some bad people in the jungle." Xeno smiled. Godarz wasn't sure whom

Xeno meant, jungle lurkers or Baktrian thugs.

"Are you no longer in King Eukratides' service, Xeno?" Godarz asked.

"We came to a parting of the ways."

"You used to deal with those that parted ways with Eukratides. How come you are still in the land of the living?"

"I don't know. I was always merciful and swift in my duties and never left anyone where they wouldn't be found and get a decent burial. I suppose I have excellent karma." Xeno smiled again. "But enough of that," his voice was gentle and Godarz knew that meant he was thinking of murder. "We know you are seeking the Kali-vraisya temple and its golden hoard. Tell us what you know. Vasudeva must have told you much. Tell us!"

"I know the way there. As much as any jungle guide or even Chandra could tell you. But you have Artabanush!" Godarz laughed. "You wouldn't bring a such a scholar as he if he hadn't learned much at the feet of Vasudeva."

The Persian smiled nervously. "The old man cast me forth. We differed on the best path to enlightenment. I learned much from the tantriks who see the distinction between god and demon is illusory as any other. But we reconciled at last. I learned certain things."

"Very well," Xeno cut off Artabanush. "I expect we can aid each other. You will come with us, Godarz."

Godarz did not think Xeno had the whole secret of the Kali-vraisya temple. Indeed, who could? If the Greeks brought Godarz along, they could use what he knew. When the time came they would kill him. Most likely Xeno would kill them all and keep the treasure for himself, Godarz thought. Either way, Godarz was marked for death. But his choices were few—there were six of them, well armed and on horseback. Escape was not possible now.

Xeno signaled for a Baktrian to offer Godarz the reins of his horse. "I swear by Zeus and by Buddha, that I shall keep faith with you as long as you keep faith with us."

"Aye, and I'll do the same," Godarz replied. *And not a second longer, you back-stabbing rogue,* he added to himself.

ONCE AGAIN Godarz went down the jungle trail. There was no sign of the Amazons or Chandra's dacoits. The sticky heat increased through the day until it became nearly intolerable. It was late in the afternoon when they reached a barely perceptible side trail. Artabanush signaled and the group moved single-file on the new track. The Baktrian thugs very carefully placed themselves behind Godarz.

The track wound into a narrow creek bed where muddy water formed stagnant pools and the stench of rotting vegetation rose. The creek bed petered out in a slimy morass. They dismounted and led their steeds. The horses that had helped them travel so fast on solid ground were now a hindrance. The beasts neighed piteously as they floundered in one mud-hole after another.

For a moment Artabanush seemed confused. He glanced at Godarz. The Tokhari avoided his eyes. Briefly he considered feigning ignorance, but as he peered into the foul depths of the swamp a shudder ran through him. This was a place of horror, where the slimy muck gripped like a strangler's hands to pull a man into its embrace of death. Better a clean death by steel than to perish in the green hell.

Very carefully Godarz looked about. He circled the group. He slipped in the mud. Swarms of gnats fed on his flesh. The Greeks grew restive and argued. Despite the heat, Godarz felt a chill. To admit he could not find the path meant he was no longer of any use. Once more he moved in a circle pattern. Once again he slipped in the treacherous mud. He put his hand out to break his fall and painfully cracked his knuckle on a stone.

Godarz cried out as he wiped the mud from the stone. It was a piece of granite, hewn into a long, narrow shape. The stone was meant to be set upright, but had fallen over in the soft muck. With a thrill, Godarz recognized what it was. The stone was a *lingam,* the sacred symbol of Shiva, consort of Kali. To Godarz the moss-eaten stone was like twelve-cubit high flaming letters in the sky.

"This way," he said. The group followed, wading waist-deep in swamp water until they felt flagstones underfoot.

The group went forward, wading through water that sometimes reached their chins. But they always kept their feet on the stones. Godarz shuddered to think who laid that path and for what reason. Weird shapes flitted through the trees and they passed heaps of stones with human skulls fitted into niches.

The path took sudden turns and they often lost it. Then they would probe with long sticks until they found the way again. Night fell hard and inky black. Even with the sticks they found they could not keep to the path. There was no place to rest so they simply stood where they were, leaning on the exhausted and agitated horses. Things fluttered in the tree branches overhead and the strange cries of jungle beasts echoed in the night.

The Baktrians spoke darkly of divs that craved human souls to carry off. It made the others nervous until Xeno cursed and slapped them. After that they lapsed into sullen silence.

"I was always too ignorant to understand Vasudeva" Godarz said to Artabanush. "But I thought he taught you the righteous path. Why are you here?"

"What Vasudeva did not understand," Artabanush replied, "Is that in a world of empty illusion, righteousness is the emptiest of illusions."

When dawn finally broke Godarz struggled to throw off the fog that wrapped his mind. Wearily they set off again. As the sun rose the path grew easier until the paving stones were free of standing water.

The trail led them into an area of solid ground. The trees grew tall and spread their canopy. Wrist-thick creepers trailed from the jungle giants, draping languorously over massive stones. Faces peered from the choking growth. The images of kings and brahmans grimaced in dementia. Faces fashioned to show the highest and noblest aspect of a race descended from the gods now leered insanely, eroded with time and the everlasting damp that rotted even stone, sloughing off layers to reveal the kernel of stark madness underneath.

As Godarz stared at the hideous gallery he realized the statues were connected. They were affixed to a massive structure that formed a huge *stupa,* a dome, entirely covered in the jungle's aggressive growth. The curving trail was simply a narrow zone free of growth around the base of the dome. Godarz studied the lay of the ground and the form of the dome. With a shock he realized it was over one hundred cubits across, more massive that the biggest temple in Benares.

"This place is a haunt of divs," mumbled one of the Baktrians. Xeno glared at him and the thug fell silent.

Godarz was about to speak when a vulture alighted in a treetop. The Tokhari looked up at the scavenger, which seemed to look back. Godarz could have sworn that the bird's eyes glinted with mocking laughter. He reached for his bow, minded to dispatch the hellish creature. The shot went wide and the vulture flapped lazily away with a derisive squawk.

"No time for hunting. We must find forage for the horses if they are to be strong enough to bear ourselves and the loot home," Xeno said.

"There's fine forage over here, Xeno," said a familiar voice. Tomyris emerged from the jungle. Parysatis and Roxane were behind her. Arrows were fitted to their bows. Godarz watched as Xeno hesitated. The Tokhari was behind him and the loyalty of the Baktrians was suspect. Godarz saw the strain on the Greek's face.

"So you are on the trail of the Kali-vraisya temple too. We should join forces. If the legends are remotely true then there is gold enough for all inside." Xeno was at his most murderously pleasant. Godarz smiled inwardly, for now it was Tomyris's turn to be uncertain. She had no way of knowing Godarz's relationship to the Greeks. She only knew she was outnumbered.

"It is no legend!" Artabanush asserted. He moved closer to Tomyris. "It is truth. I learned many things from Vasudeva." The tone of the Persian's voice was strange and seemed to echo unpleasantly in Godarz's ears. "You must know that your best interest lies in helping us. Let yourself be guided by our wisdom. Therein lies safety."

Tomyris stared. Her face was slack and colorless. The woman's eyes showed fear and uncertainty. Then Parysatis lowered her bow and stepped close to Tomyris. She touched Tomyris's arm gently and spoke a single word in her ear.

Tomyris snarled and her eyes blazed. She loosed an arrow that passed within a hair of Artabanush's head.

"Don't ever try that again, or the next time my arrow will split your black heart!" She turned with a scornful toss of her head and kissed Parysatis tenderly.

"I'll keep him in check, Tomyris," Xeno said nervously. "Do we still have a deal?"

"Enough of one, but see that you keep it scrupulously!"

THE GROUP cooperated in a surly fashion. The horses were watered and turned out to graze in an open spot the Amazons had found. Godarz and the Baktrians erected a corral of thorny brushwood, more to keep the steeds from wandering than to deter the voracious tigers that hunted in the jungle. Then the treasure-seekers fed themselves and rested. The passage of the swamp had taxed them greatly and they would need all their strength to face the temple.

"What do you actually know of the temple, besides the way here?" Xeno asked of Tomyris.

"We learned enough among the holy men at Benares to start us on the trail. We hoped to learn more from Vasudeva himself. He knew more about the Kali-vraisya than any other man living, more than any man in generations. You should know you have his former student and his friend." Tomyris shot a venomous look at Artabanush and Godarz. "But he died before we could reach him. Instead we tracked down one of his disciples who had turned hermit and was living in the Paropamisus Mountains. He cursed us for devil-temptresses trying to lead him astray. As if! We camped in front of his cave. Naturally we exercised to keep fit in the high altitude and we did so Greek style, nude. We ran, wrestled, stretched, and anointed each other with oil. He talked and we took our leave of the lecherous old prig. You'd think he would have thanked us for leaving his sanctity intact. But gratitude from a *saddhu* is rarer than honesty in a Greek or wits in a Tokhari."

"Whatever he told you was rubbish," Artabanush said. "Your only hope is to follow our lead. Only I have all the routes of the subterranean chambers memorized. Vasudeva taught me, Ohrmazd keep his soul. Wander off on your own and death awaits. The builders of the temple knew how to guard their treasure."

Roxane laughed mirthlessly. "Death awaits us anyway. Tomyris, you know what the hermit warned us about. There are legends, this is no treasure vault built by Rama of Ayodhya. What need had he of gold? Old Ayodha had enough that they made the children's toys of it. His treasure was Queen Sita. King Rama battled divs, rakshasas, and demons for her." Roxane glanced at Artabanush. "Some say that those he did not slay he imprisoned here. And he laid traps to slay such fools as might tamper with that which lies within."

Artabanush made as if to silence the Amazon, but she carried on recklessly. "Do I come to close to the bone, Persian? You should know of such things. When you ran with Pseosiris, you boasted of your mastery of the unseen world."

Parysatis looked around. "Pseosiris? The black sorcerer who made a stir at the court of King Seleukis? Wasn't he poisoned?"

Roxane paid her no heed. "Rakshasas, they lurk in graveyards, feeding on death and corruption. They can take the form of dogs or scavenger birds, aye and fouler things too. Their very malevolence is enough to warp all that comes into contact with their unspeakable essence."

Xeno made a sign to ward off the evil eye. "Enough! If you dare not seek the gold, turn back! But I keep your supplies." He glowered at the Amazons. Godarz sensed nerves were strained to the breaking point by the fear of rakshasas and greed for loot.

"We dare!" Tomyris answered. Her Amazons might carp and complain but Godarz knew her word was law.

Artabanush led them all to a section of blank wall flanked by two grotesque faces. Xeno called them gorgons, but they were more than that. Images of fiendishness meant to frighten fiends. They were not Greek, nor yet Indian, but something older, something that whispered secrets long forgotten and tales better left untold.

Artabanush told the Baktrians to cut away the brush and creepers that masked the wall. When it was clear Artabanush recited a curious verse,

In the fertile field between
The Kirittmukha, faces of glory.
Ascend as the Maruts,
Proud warriors of the sky,
Seven in number.
They made the journey,
Three days to the sacred soma.

While he spoke, Artabanush counted seven stones from the bottom and three across from the gorgon masks. At the intersection Artabanush marked the stone and, drawing a small hammer from his pack, prepared to smash it.

Godarz knew he should keep silent, but he had pledged good faith to Xeno. "Stop!" he said. The Tokhari pointed to the stone projection that supported the left-hand gorgon face. He spoke a verse too.

Take the right hand path
And the Face of Glory
Gives a blessing.
On the left the dragon
Virta, the dragon's fangs
Spew poison.

Godarz took a blanket from his bedroll. Carefully he laid it over the left-hand gorgon. "Continue," he said.

Artabanush smashed the stone and reached into a hollow that was revealed. He gripped a bronze lever and pulled mightily. The Persian groaned and strained and the rod gave way. The stonework tumbled inward to reveal an entrance into the dome. At the same time the blanket started violently. An arrowhead protruded from it, a hair's breadth from Artabanush's hand. He knelt by it and sniffed. "Poisoned, or I'm a Syrian eunuch."

"You'd know poison, my friend," Xeno commented.

"How did it stay fresh all this time?" Parysatis asked.

"Anything will keep fresh if tightly sealed." Lykaeon said. "I knew a Cappodocian tomb robber who found a jug of wine in a king's grave that was still drinkable after a thousand years."

"What did he do with it?" Parysatis asked.

"Nothing. Someone wanted his share so they stuck a knife in the Cappodocian's back and left him dead in an alley. Tomb robbers are all back-stabbing scum." Lykaeon whistled a happy tune as the group lit torches and entered the temple.

THERE WAS a short passageway broad enough to allow two abreast. The passage terminated in a bronze–bound door. The oak was rotten with age and the bronze had become a mass of fused verdigris. No one could offer any verse that warned of a trap so they warily opened it. The group filed into a larger chamber. Two doorways exited from that room. At a sign from Artabanush they chose the left hand one. They mounted stairs that led up into the dome, then descended again. They entered and exited rooms, seemingly at random. At last they entered one where the thick dust of age had been disturbed by many feet.

"May the rakshasas take you!" Lykaeon exclaimed. With a curse he drew his sword and turned on the Amazons. "The Amazons have let in the dacoits! They are in league with Chandra!" The Amazons reached for their weapons.

Godarz knew his life hung by a thread. Neither the Amazons nor the Greeks trusted him. In a fight he was on his own. "Wait!" he cried. Puzzled, the group hesitated. Godarz bent down and studied the tracks by torchlight. He was raised to hunt wild cattle on the open steppes; he knew tracks told a tale to those who could read. "Yes," he drawled, "I think Tomyris and the girls have kept faith. Unless Chandra's gang have taken to wearing Skythian boots." Godarz carefully matched each set of tracks to its owner, finishing with his own.

"Hades's black heart!" Xeno hissed. "You've led us in a circle you Persian dolt!"

Artabanush stammered excuses. "The temple is designed to be circled! We merely missed a mark. There is a *mandala* we must find! I know, Vasudeva wrote of it in the scroll I had from him!"

Xeno silenced the Persian with a savage blow and a curse. But Godarz had heard Artabanush. He thought of the strange disarray of Vasudeva's library. The old sage taught by the word, though he read such writings as wise men kept. Godarz recalled Vasudeva had told him of a mandala in a stupa, the sacred plan of the world enclosed in the cosmic dome. Vasudeva had drawn the figure for him once. He traced the design.

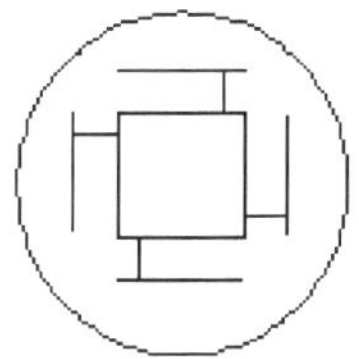

"The temple isn't marked with a mandala—it is the mandala. There is a central room with flanking galleries, enclosed in the dome," Godarz concluded.

Roxane spoke, "Two turnings back we passed through a corridor of slightly greater width. By my reckoning it ran east-west. Perhaps it had a hidden passage into the central chamber."

They back-tracked to the corridor Roxane spoke of. They entered from the east end. Godarz and the Amazons had a sense of direction and motion honed by life on the trackless plains and they agreed they were in the southern third of the vast temple dome. Artabanush rushed past them to the far corner of the room.

"A maker's mark, etched in the stone!" he cried. "We missed it before." He hung his torch in a bracket on the wall and studied the mark closely. "The mark, it is a mandala!"

"Hush!" Tomyris hissed. "I hear voices."

Godarz listened, the beating of his heart seemed loud enough to be heard a mile away. Then voices came to him. The sound was muted, filtered through the maze of corridors. Or was it nearby, a single voice that whispered, "Death!"

"The dacoits," Tomyris muttered. "They followed us in." She started toward the entrance to the gallery. Parysatis and Roxane followed. Godarz hesitated between the Amazons and Xeno's gang.

As he hesitated, he heard a sound from the corner. Artabanush gave a cry of triumph. Simultaneously a harsh grating noise sounded overhead. A massive bronze grate crashed to the floor. Only Godarz's cat-like reflexes saved him from being crushed like an olive in a press. He found himself shut into the west half of the gallery with Xeno and his men. The Amazons were on the other side of the gate.

Xeno laughed. "Another trap of the ancients. Alas, we have been separated and must part ways." A bronze door stood open in the corner. It had a thin stone face that mimicked the wall. Xeno and his men backed up to it, swords and bows at the ready.

"What of the Tokhari?" asked Lykaeon.

"We have no need of him. The scroll Artabanush stole from Vasudeva will tell us how to find the loot. By Zeus, the old fool sickened me with his prating of Buddha and the noble path. I'm glad you poisoned the senseless babbler, Artabanush!"

"I'll have your heart's blood for that!" Godarz roared. With a tigerish leap he whipped out his sword and rushed Xeno's thugs.

The Baktrians dropped their torches and began to shoot arrows at the Amazons. The women shot back and arrows flew wildly between the groups in the uncertain light. Godarz could see Xeno's gang were crowding through the hidden door, but were hindered by their numbers.

In the flickering shadows a body crashed into Godarz and he found himself battling a Baktrian. Sparks flew from their swords as they clashed. Godarz stepped aside as the Baktrian slashed wildly. Godarz hit back, nearly blind in the dark. He felt his blade crush armor and bite into flesh. The Baktrian groaned in agony and his shadowy form crumbled.

Frenzied with killing, Godarz leapt at the retreating shapes. He blundered into a man. At close range Godarz recognized Artabanush. The Tokahari raised his sword to cut him down, but the Persian muttered a mantra and slapped Godarz lightly on the arm. Instantly Godarz's right side was shot through with pain. His sword dropped from nerveless hands and he sagged to his knees. Madness clawed at Godarz's mind; hell had taken him in life. Through searing jets of agony he raised his left hand and clutched at Artabanush's hand. The sorcerer laughed and pushed him away. Godarz was left alone, but he still gripped something in his hand.

The Tokahari groaned in pain as he staggered to his feet. An arrow skipped off his armor.

"May the divs take you! Why are you still trying to kill me?" he bellowed at the Amazons.

"Sorry," came the reply.

Godarz stumbled toward the secret door. It was closed. As Godarz fumbled at it he heard a bolt click home on the other side. He raged inwardly. He would track Xeno and his scum to the Pillars of Harakles and beyond to make them pay for killing Vasudeva. The pain had subsided and he could use his right arm again. Godarz had no idea how Artabanush had caused such agony with a touch, but speculation crawled though his mind like a venomous serpent. Rumor called the Persian a black sorcerer and some said that was why Vasudeva had dismissed him. With a shudder of horror, Godarz realized the rumors were true.

THE AMAZONS recovered a torch from the floor and studied the bronze gate. The Baktrian lay still in a pool of blood.

Roxane groaned. "This is a place of evil. It was built on blood and walled in with a curse. We should leave."

"Enough," Tomyris replied. "Let us raise the gate and release Godarz." She turned to him. "Tokhari, I misjudged you. I apologize."

Godarz nodded. Then he remembered the thing he clutched in his hand. He showed it to the Amazons and it glinted in the torchlight. It was Artabanush's silver ring. Carefully Godarz tugged at it. The top slipped to one side and revealed a green powder. "Now we know how Artabanush killed Vasudeva." He cast the ring aside.

Suddenly a light flared at the entrance to the gallery. Four dacoits stalked in, swords and bows at the ready. "Kill them!" they shouted.

The Amazons whirled to face the invaders. Godarz was still cut off by the bronze gate. He drew his bow and backed up to have room to shoot.

Suddenly he felt a chill pass through him as though someone had trod upon his grave or whispered his name in the halls of the dead. He heard the curses and shouts of the dacoits and Amazons but dimly. An iron-hard hand, cold as death, clutched his arm. Godarz whirled to face it and looked into the eyes of the dead Baktrian.

Godarz's senses reeled. He had killed the Baktrian, but the man still lived. He was covered in blood and Godarz could see bone protruding from the gash in his chest. The dead thing's eyes blazed with insane hate and lust for killing. Godarz dropped his bow and reached for his sword with a cat-like motion. But the thing hurled the warrior aside as if he were a rag doll.

The dead Baktrian shambled forward to the bronze gate. As Godarz leapt to his feet the thing grabbed the bars and pulled them apart. The Amazons and dacoits paused in their battle to face the newcomer. Parysatis gasped in horror and even the dacoits recoiled from the bloody thing that stalked them.

One of the dacoits rushed the dead man. The bandit slashed him with his sword. But the thing did not fall. He gave a horrible, ghastly laugh that rang like a soul in the lowest pit of Hell. With incredible swiftness the thing seized the dacoit. He sunk his teeth into the bandit's throat and tore it out in a welter of blood.

The Amazons and dacoits backed away and shot their arrows into the thing. Still he did not fall, but stalked forward. The dacoits were closest to the door and crowded through it, screaming as they fled. The Baktrian whirled and advanced on the Amazons, trying to push them against the bronze grate, showing a diabolic intent under insensate blood-lust.

Godarz shadowed the fiend, for he knew it was not a man. Though his very soul revolted at the thought of coming near it, he lunged and stabbed his sword entirely into the thing's back. The blade wedged fast in its backbone and was wrenched from Godarz's hands. Burning eyes turned on Godarz with the speed of a cobra and clutched him. The Tokhari struggled with all his strength to hold off the beast that hissed and gibbered in a strange tongue. Its snapping teeth drew closer.

From behind, Roxane loomed from the shadows. She struck a heavy blow and cried, "In the name of Kali die!" Instantly the thing collapsed like a puppet with its strings cut.

Godarz gasped for breath and Roxane lent him a supporting arm. Parysatis stared at the Baktrian's corpse. "He was shamming." Her voice was small, like a child who is frightened of the dark.

"By Ohrmazd, Zeus, and Buddha, no! I killed him the first time!" Godarz shouted.

"We go," said Tomyris.

THEY FLED through the corridors back to the temple's entrance. "I'll lie in wait and slay Xeno when he emerges," Godarz muttered.

"If he emerges," Roxane answered.

They neared the vestibule at the entrance to the temple. "Stop," Tomyris commanded. There was a light ahead and men were crowding into the corridor. At their head was a tall, handsome man with a bristling mustache and a topknot that gleamed with a golden band. He wore Hindi armor of leather bands and held an Indian short-sword, the kind with the broad tip that could shear off a limb with a single blow. "Chandra! The men we fought were but his scouts." Tomyris groaned.

"Slay the Amazons!" Chandra roared.

Godarz realized that Chandra too had adopted the tactic of waiting to kill whomsoever emerged, like a cat sitting at a mouse-hole. They would find Godarz was no mouse though.

One dacoit sprang ahead of the others. Godarz feinted to his head and then reversed the blow and cut the man's leg out from under him. The other dacoits hung back and shot arrows.

"Too many, let's go!" Tomyris shouted. They ran, but the dacoits' blood was up and they pursued. At corners the Amazons turned and fired arrows, but the bandits shot back and forced their prey to flee onward.

Through the grim and maze-like corridors the chase continued until Godarz lost all sense of direction. At last Parysatis panted, "I think we've lost them."

"Aye, and ourselves," Tomyris replied.

"No, look," Godarz gestured at the room they were in. It was a gallery like the one where they had parted company with Xeno. Swiftly they hunted for sign of the secret door.

"How do we know the ceiling won't fall on us or poisoned spears won't stab us when we open the door?" Parysatis asked gloomily.

"We don't," Tomyris replied with a shrug.

Roxane found the mark of the mandala. Further searching revealed a hidden latch. With trepidation, she opened it. A bronze door, faced with stone, swung open. They stood, counting their heartbeats. Nothing happened.

"The ancients must have left one way open," Parysatis said.

As she spoke a massive stone block fell from the ceiling by the entrance. It hit the ground with a resounding crash.

"But they hated anyone who tried to leave," Roxane said.

They entered the passage they had opened. A short, narrow corridor led to another bronze door. That door let onto a large square room. Godarz knew they were at the heart of the mandala.

Oil lamps set in niches along the wall had been lit. They revealed a central stone altar. The altar had images of the Hindu gods, Indra and Brahma, Vishnu and Shiva, graven on its surface. On opposite walls were images of Kali and Shiva. Elsewhere the symbols of the lingam and the trident were inscribed. But the most striking object in the room was the corpse of a man, lying in a pool of blood. It was one of the Baktrians, dead from a terrible gash in his head.

"They must have quarreled and killed him," Tomyris said.

"Where do we go from here?" Roxane asked.

Godarz merely pointed at the altar and the footprints in the dust that circled it. Tomyris knelt and studied them closely. Finally she said, "It pivots. I can see its track. One stands thus," and she pushed aside the corpse of the Baktrian. "Then you grip the bosses on the stone thus and push." She grasped the altar, lightly it seemed to Godarz, but the great stone slipped aside, pivoting away at a mere touch.

Parysatis leapt forward and hurled Tomyris to the ground. As she did a great bronze blade flashed from the shadows that shrouded the ceiling. It whipped through the air exactly where Tomyris had been standing. The altar continued its motion, revealing, briefly, a hole in the floor under it. Then the altar rolled back into place, from within the floor came the sound of clanking chains and gears. The blade continued its swing and stopped with a click, loaded for the next person who should approach the altar.

"Nicely counter-weighted. Menander had a Greek from Syracuse who could design things like that." Roxane's voice mingled fear and wonder.

Tomyris gave Parysatis a kiss. "At least we know to duck when we push at the thing."

"No," Godarz replied. "That's not it. I remember a mantra Vasudeva used to say. It ran, 'At the center of the mandala, give reverence to the gods, Indra, Brahma, Vishnu, Shiva."

"Wasn't Vasudeva a Buddhist?" Parysatis asked. "Why would he give a Greek's wet loincloth about the gods of the Hindus?"

"Doubtless, he wanted to kill me." Godarz knelt by the altar. Muttering Vasudeva's mantra, he touched the images of the gods, one each side of the great square. One by one, they rocked back with a click. Indra, Brahma, Vishnu, and Shiva last. A metallic clang resounded from inside the altar. Godarz pushed and the altar rolled away smoothly. The bronze blade stayed in place. Silently the group descended into the chasm below the altar. Godarz repressed a shudder at the thought of how the wound in the rock resembled an open grave.

THE FISSURE went down a long way. Bronze handholds had been affixed to the rock and a hollow space hacked from the stone and filled with chains and weights that operated the trap on the altar. More disturbing were the repeated images of Kali, in her most grotesque and violent aspect and the bizarre ways they had been disfigured. The bottom was lost in darkness; they could only tell it went a long way. No one could climb that ladder and hold a torch, so they doused the light and began their descent.

The group worked their way down the rungs, sweating and cursing as their weapons and armor continually caught on the rungs or projecting bits of stone. They climbed in absolute darkness, feeling cautiously for the rungs or handholds in the rock and praying to all the gods that they not slip and fall to a certain death.

Godarz wasn't sure how long they had been descending when Roxane cried out. "What is it?" they all asked at once.

"Wings. I felt the brush of a wing on my face and saw eyes glaring at me from the dark."

"You're going soft in the head," Tomyris snarled. "It was a bat." But Godarz wasn't sure, for he too sensed something in the dark. There was a voice, barely audible, that hissed and snarled and seemed to speak of dread secrets in a language not intended for the human tongue. He did not speak of it.

At last they reached the bottom of the ladder and put their feet on solid ground. Roxane rekindled the torch with her flint and steel. They found themselves in an irregular tunnel, about five to seven feet high and just wide enough for two abreast. In places massive timbers shored the tunnel. Water dripped and trickled down the walls where strange cave molds bloomed into hideous and mocking shapes. They moved forward in the flickering torchlight and the mix of smoke and dank that seared the lungs.

Godarz took the lead. The floor was paved with irregularly shaped slabs of rock that sometimes shifted underfoot. Plodding forward they passed a narrow fissure in the rock. It was a vertical split in the wall on their left and it was as broad as a man's forearm. Godarz gave it a searching glance, but could see nothing save blank darkness. Indeed, he could see little at all for the smoke stung his eyes till they watered. The passage of the swamp, repeated battle, and the brooding horror of the maze had worn him down. Wearily, he moved forward. Roxane followed, holding the torch. Tomyris was next and Parysatis covered the rear.

Godarz stepped on a stone that seemed particularly loose. For a moment he hesitated. Then from behind him came a snarl and a cry of surprise. Godarz whirled to see Xeno and his thugs emerging from the crack in the wall. Xeno had his arm locked about Parysatis's throat. The Amazon struggled in his grasp while he sought to thrust a sword through a gap in her armor.

Tomyris hurled herself at Xeno, only to find she could not strike her foe without hitting her lover. Godarz held his ground as the stone rolled drunkenly under his feet. Roxane stepped next to him, seeking to unite their force. With gut-wrenching suddenness the stone slab up-ended. Godarz could hear screaming, and dirt and pebbles pelted his face. He fell into a pit, crashed against its sides as stones tore at his armor and flesh. He hit bottom in a heap and Roxane landed on him. Dirt cascaded around them, covering their limbs and faces. Madly, Godarz scrambled from under her, dragging at her hand. A grinding wail announced the stone slab had torn free. Convulsively Godarz pushed away from the pit's center. He felt an agonizing pain in his leg as the massive stone struck him.

HE LAY in the dark, seeing absolutely nothing. He could feel dirt, rock and Roxane's body pressed close to him on all sides. "Roxane, do you live?"

"I do, Godarz," she answered.

Godarz struggled. "My leg is pinned. I can not reach it." Roxane twisted to scrape at the dirt and rock. As she dug Godarz felt his leg come free. It was trapped more by the rubble than the great slab, which had wedged itself in the pit just barely above the bottom. Still the pain in Godarz's limb was intense.

Exploring by feel Godarz found they were in a hollow space below the pit trap. It was just of a size for both to lie side by side and formed part of another tunnel. Godarz's face was oriented to the tunnel so he could snake forward. The tube was just wide enough for one person to wriggle through. Godarz had a nauseating image of a jungle python, long and sleek, but with a disgusting bulge where the serpent was digesting its prey.

It was impossible to turn around or to climb up past the stone, so they began to crawl through the tunnel. The way was agonizing. They were cramped and contorted. The darkness was palpable and suffocating. Godarz could not see the stones that he cracked his head against, he had lost his helmet in the fall and soon blood was flowing freely down his face. Even worse were the showers of dirt and pebbles that he dislodged, tiny falls that sadistically hinted of a greater collapse. In every heartbeat he endured an unending death of burial alive.

A ghastly howl welled up from the bowels of the earth. Godarz dared to face anything living over sharp steel, but there in that living grave his blood ran cold and he knew fear.

Again came the howl, a pitiful wail of hate and pain. It was a moan filled with grave-rot and leprosy, a scream of insensate hate, fury, and demented cunning. It was the cry of a diseased pariah dog that digs at graves in the night and feeds on the rotting flesh therein.

Godarz and Roxane lay close by each other in the tunnel, scarcely able to move. Panic gripped Roxane's voice as she spoke. "In the name of the gods, I must have light or I will go mad!"

From behind Godarz a light flared up. He writhed onto his side so he could look back down the tunnel. Roxane had used her flint and steel to light a bit of tinder. The burning tow revealed Roxane lying on her belly in the tunnel. Beyond her, Godarz could see the face of a dog, hideous, rabid and baring its fangs.

The tinder burned out and darkness returned. Roxane screamed. The beast snarled. Godarz heard its jaws snap.

Frantically Godarz tried to squeeze back down the tunnel to help Roxane. She was screaming hysterically. Godarz's armor tore at her as he compressed himself alongside. Every second was a torment crushed in that tiny space. He felt the hell-hound bite him and he kicked at it again and again. He blindly smashed his foot into the fiend's face. He kicked something very solid that jarred his already injured leg. Suddenly a wave of dirt and stones buried his legs and feet. The hell-hound was buried but so were Godarz and Roxane's legs.

The cave-in was not packed tight and Godarz could pull his limbs free. Godarz forced himself back up the tunnel. From behind he heard a ghastly scratching sound. His strength was spent. Exhausted by battle and nearly suffocated he could crawl only a little farther. Grimly he pushed his arms forward to feel the way ahead. They encountered a large rock that blocked the tunnel completely. Godarz let out a sob as he realized this was the end. They would die in the darkness.

"Roxane?"

"I live," she answered feebly.

"We can go no further. There is a rock. By the merciful Buddha I had not thought to die like a rat in a trap. Maybe my next life will be better. I'll listen better to Vasudeva next time." Godarz was drained, he felt only a self-pity that longed for death.

"Better that, than in the belly of a div." Roxane groaned. "Oh, for a dagger to end this."

From behind Godarz heard the scratching again. Anger welled inside of him. He would not avenge Vasudeva, instead he would be carrion in a pit for devils. He pushed at the stone, but it would not budge. He felt his heart about to burst and his head swam. All was blackness.

THE TOKHARI was not sure where he was. His body had expanded to a vast and shadowy bulk. The absolute darkness of the pit was shot through with light. All sense of up, down, left, and right was gone. Godarz was floating in a void.

Then Godarz heard a voice. It was strangely familiar. "What do you desire warrior?" it said.

"To live, to have revenge," Godarz answered. He felt a presence that commanded his attention. Something in him stirred, with the unease of an animal in the presence of the unknown.

"Those will not advance your enlightenment. Maybe it were better to die now."

Godarz knew who was speaking.

"I'll come back and wring your next incarnation's chicken-neck, Vasudeva."

"Maybe it wouldn't advance your enlightenment to die now. You might live, my friend, and achieve your revenge, though I utterly disavow any desire for it. Revenge is no part of dharma. I died nearly enlightened, which is the best I could hope for in this life. My attachments to things led me into many errors. Artabanush was one.

"Listen, Godarz, once Artabanus sat at my knee to hear

wisdom. I swelled with pride that someone had come so far to hear the pearls of wisdom I let fall. I was the greatest fool of all! I found I had fed a viper who would bite.

"You may put an end to his time, but that will not free you from the cycle of re-birth. But you might learn something of this land and the secrets it harbors. Use that wisdom well. You may serve to keep others from blotting their karma worse than they already have. Reject Illusion. Sometimes we strive to push away things we should draw to us. Goodbye, Godarz."

Godarz listened, but the voice was gone; he heard the scratching behind him. He felt the tunnel press in on his pain-wracked body. Roxane's breath was coming in gasps, she would die soon. He reached for the stone. His fingers explored its surface again. As they reached the edge, he felt small hollows that he could grip. Godarz pulled with the last of his strength and the stone came away.

Godarz saw a lighted chamber ahead. Fresh air wafted out. He was strong enough to pull himself in. Despite the pain that wracked his every bone and joint, he turned around and reached for Roxane. She revived at his touch and together they crawled into a womb in the rock.

They found themselves in a small natural hollow in the bedrock. Fragments of crystal reflected the eerie glow of a type of cave moss that produced its own phosphorescent light. On opposite sides of the cave the images of Shiva and Parvati had been carved. Between the Holy Ones was a hollow in the floor where water collected. Greedily, Godarz and Roxane flung themselves at it.

The water was sweet and pure. Filtered by the limestone and mingled with the peculiar cave-moss, it was immaculate and divine. They drank until thirst was gone and cleansed away the filth and blood that clung to them and they knew this was *soma*, the very drink of the gods. Weariness pulled Godarz's limbs down. He had stripped off his armor as had Roxane. Suddenly he found her, naked and nestled in his arms. He admired her, her breasts were firm and high and her legs were long. Though she was well curved, the strength in her young frame was evident, as were the battle scars that marked her here and there. Her breath came in the slow steady rhythm of sleep.

AS GODARZ sank into sleep too, he looked at the images on the wall. How Shiva's eyes seemed to flash at him. Or was that a trick of the mossy witch-light on Lord Shiva's crystalline eyes? Godarz glanced at Parvati, the divine bride of Shiva. The Hindus knew her as an avatar of Kali, the war goddess. Was it Godarz's sleep-fogged brain that made Parvati suddenly show cruel fangs and a bloody sword? Or that her features reminded him of a woman, with raven hair and ice blue eyes?

Godarz slept deeply. He dreamt of lives lived in other times. Sometimes he was a blond-haired giant with a bloody axe, and other times a slim dark man who moved with the grace of a cat through nameless cities. Still other times he strode a deck and heard thunder issue from metal pillars with great gouts of flame and hurtling balls. Yet again he was a stocky, slant-eyed man astride a shaggy pony. Another time his long black hair was decorated with feathers and he held a steel tube and waited for men in blue coats to come and do battle.

And each time he saw a woman, sometimes by his side, other times only as a dream in the dream-lives he lived. Always she was the force that moved him, restless through the world.

The dream-lives came faster and faster till they were no more than a blur. Godarz felt a sense of motion, a fast, forward swooping. Then he was aloft, high over the dome of the Kali-vraisya temple, winging over the jungle. Roxane was by his side. Together they hurtled over the trees, the sun-baked plains, the hills and verdant valleys, over a sea of jumbled stone and snow, higher than any bird to the very peaks of the mountains.

In a limpid blue sky a massive temple sat on the crest of a mountain. Gardens surrounded it and deer grazed contentedly. Godarz saw the temple was shaped like a mandala, below the stupa-dome of Heaven itself. The doors of the temple flew open. Godarz and Roxane entered and knelt before Shiva and Parvati.

Godarz bowed down before the gods. And when he looked up, he saw not Parvati but Kali, hideous and athirst for blood.

"Which shall it be daughter?" she said to Roxane.

"I yearn for peace, but if I must I will wade through a river of blood to get there," the Amazon replied.

"Peace shall be yours," Kali said, and she extended a fearful blessing.

Shiva pointed to the jungle and Godarz was striding under the trees. And he was not Godarz, but Rama, prince of Ayodhya. And lovely Sita walked at his side.

From the depths of the jungle, foul things slithered. The Rakshasa horde vomited forth, their hideous shapes polluted the land. Filled with hatred, cruelty and lust they swarmed about Rama and Sita. They bit and clawed at the prince and his bride.

"Rama!" the Rakshasas howled, "Give us your gold to enjoy and your woman to ravish and we will spare your life. Aye, we will let ye worship us, ye crawling mortal!" And the fiends gibbered and raved of the unspeakable horrors they would visit on the just and unjust alike.

Sita recoiled in horror, but Rama laughed a quiet laugh and picked up his sword. Where Rama's sword passed, a hundred heads fell. Then a strange light came into Sita's eyes and she laughed a Kali-laugh and picked up a sword. And where Sita's sword passed a hundred heads fell.

They cut down the vulture-Rakshasas who flapped filthy wings and breathed carrion breath. They slew the dog-Rakshasas who dripped madness from their fangs. They slaughtered the corpse-Rakshasas who danced madly in cemeteries making use of bodies that were not their own. Together Rama and Sita slew the Rakshasas, until even they grew sick with the rivers of diseased blood and the mangled corpses. At last only one Rakshasa was left and it cried out for mercy.

"Spare me, oh Rama! Spare me, oh Sita!"

Sita nodded to Rama. "We shall spare ye, foul demon, for mercy belongs to the gods and we fear lest, on this day of slaughter, we slay mercy too."

"But ye shall be bound forever here," Rama added. "And no longer may ye go abroad to work your evil." So saying Rama summoned servitors, the Yakshasa folk, who made obeisance to him, though the Yakshasas were nigh kin to the gods. With strange arts they built the Kali-vraisya temple.

"You lusted for gold to sate your greed and beauty to sate your desire. You shall have them. They are the bed ye made, lie in it!" And Rama caused a great stone sarcophagus to be made in the crypt below the temple. It was carved with the images of nameless and forgotten gods. In it he put jewels of great beauty and much gold. The Rakshasa was laid in it and Rama sealed the sarcophagus with a seal shaped like a mandala set in a stupa.

"As long as the seal shall last, your evil spirit is bound to this place," Rama said. There would be other battles with the Rakshasas. Many still lurked over the sea on the island of Lanka and lusted for revenge. But for now they were defeated.

When Rama and Sita's labors were done, they purified themselves. Together they celebrated the Vraisya rite in honor of Kali. With passionate embraces they celebrated the rite. And the jungle heard gasps of delight and the wild bull snorted in pleasure.

GODARZ AWOKE wrapped in Roxane's embrace. Their bodies moved rhythmically together. The warrior and the Amazon groaned in ecstasy and were silent a while. Godarz was refreshed and renewed. The weariness and pain that had hung on him like shackles were gone. His muscular limbs glistened in the witch-glow of the cave. Roxane stretched her perfect body, lithe and full of vigor.

"Sita," he said.

"Rama," she replied.

They said no more but went about dressing and donning their armor, which gleamed golden and seemed strangely lacking in damage. Their swords and bows were at hand. Armed, they went out through a crack in the wall of the rock-womb. They found themselves in an upward-sloping passage.

They mounted higher until they reached a regular staircase. They climbed on effortlessly as if their bodies were not their own.

Godarz realized his senses were keyed to an unnatural pitch. Though they had no light, he could see the way. He glanced back at Roxane. She seemed different to him, as though she were something more than the Amazon he had met in Gandhara. In her face and movement he saw something of Sita and something of Kali too. The mingling of bride and destroyer was at once strange and natural to Godarz.

Something else reached Godarz's heightened senses. It was the sound of a woman sobbing silently.

At the head of the stairs they found Tomyris. She was slumped in a heap on the floor. As Godarz and Roxane approached she sat up gripping her sword.

"Who is it? Man or div I care not! Xeno has taken my one true love and not all the Rakshasas in hell will keep me from Parysatis. If you bar my way I will slay you, for I have sworn to slay Xeno ere I die!"

"It is Roxane, sister." The Amazon's voice was gentle yet filled with a rich tone that Godarz had never heard before. "Follow us and we shall lead you to Parysatis."

Tomyris followed them as they threaded maze-like corridors. Never once did Godarz hesitate at a turning or a fork. It did not seem strange to him that he should know the way. Had he not been present when the great edifice was built?

They turned a corner and entered a chamber. It was lit by torches, yet was still so big that the corners were lost in shadows. On the far side was another entrance. Xeno and his gang were clustered about a great sarcophagus. Parysatis lay bound on the floor. Godarz recognized the carvings on the sarcophagus, the leering faces of demented gods and demons. As Godarz watched, the Baktrian pried apart the seal left by Rama. The gang heaved the covering slab aside. It fell to the floor with a mighty crash. The sarcophagus revealed its treasure: gold and jewels in riotous profusion.

"Dogs! You seal your doom by opening that!" Godarz roared.

"Back or I slice the wench's throat!" Xeno hissed, his sword pressed tight to Parysatis's throat.

"Slice and be damned! All of you drop your weapons! The loot belongs to Chandra and his bold dacoits!" From out of the opposite doorway Godarz saw the dacoits pour forth. There were a dozen of them and at their head stood Chandra.

THE THREE hostile groups held their ground, hesitating before committing to a bloody battle that would end with the complete extermination of the vanquished.

Then Godarz heard a soul-freezing howl. He had heard it before in the very pits of the temple. He had heard it when the Rakshasas fought Rama. Now he saw its source. From out of the shadows in the far corner of the room it took shape. In form it was neither a vulture, nor a diseased dog, nor yet a putrescent corpse, but a hideous thing that combined all three and shambled upright when it should crawl on its belly.

"Indra and Brahma! What in the name of all the gods is that?" Chandra goggled at the fiend.

"Free! Finally I am free! How I shall savor my liberty. Oh, to lay waste to the lands under the sun! I shall throw down the images of the gods! Worship me and I shall teach you unholy rites. The most obscene pleasures imaginable we shall sample in the very temples of the gods!" The Rakshasa raved and gibbered as it described the horrors it would commit.

Chandra hurled a curse at the fiend. He pointed his sword and the dacoit bowmen feathered the demon with shafts. The Rakshasa laughed a jackal laugh and caught the nearest dacoit's arm. As easily as one tears a piece of bread, it ripped apart the bandit into bloody rags.

Artabanush fell to his knees and cried out, "Oh master, I worship thee! I am yours to command!'

The Rakshasa pointed a gore-dripping talon at Godarz. "Slay him! He is the very one that imprisoned me here!"

All at once the melee erupted. Chandra's dacoits gave

ground before the Rakshasa, desperately trying to injure the fiend while staying out of reach of its deadly grasp. But Chandra's men were panicky and only the resolute stand of their leader held them together.

Xeno tried to flee, but found himself blocked by Tomyris. Sword on sword, they clashed in furious combat. Roxane rushed to Parysatis's side but Lykaeon and the Baktrian met her and pressed the Amazon back with fanatical fury. She held them at bay, fighting as one possessed.

Artabanush leapt at Godarz like a madman. He moaned a mantra and raised his open hand to strike. A pale nimbus showed about the sorcerer's hand and Godarz knew it had the power to strike one dead. The Persian's terrible hand of death flashed downward like a thunderbolt, but Godarz whipped his sword up with lightning speed. Artabanush's hand went spinning away in a spurt of blood.

"I strike, not to avenge Vasudeva, but that ye may work no more evil!" Godarz struck again and Artabanush's head flew from his shoulders.

A crazed dacoit cut down the Baktrian from behind. The madman hurled himself at Roxane. She stabbed him half a dozen times before he fell. Lykaeon's nerve broke and he fled the Amazon, only to run straight into the Rakshasa. The Greek's end was frightful.

Tomyris was still engaged against Xeno. Godarz was stalking the Rakshasa and could offer no help. Roxane freed Parysatis from her bonds and turned to aid Godarz against the demon. The dacoits had broken and were fleeing the beast. All except one, Chandra scuttled to the sarcophagus and plunged his hands into the heaped treasure. He scooped up a rajah's ransom and started to work his way out of the chamber of death.

A voice came from Godarz, but ever afterward he swore it was not his own. He never said who spoke, but he knew the voice from his dream.

"I spared you once. But in their greed, these fools have made a battle to the death inevitable."

"You are the fool to have shown mercy, for I have none," the Rakshasa sneered. "Die now!"

The Rakshasa leapt on Godarz, tearing and biting. Roxane hewed at its flank though it took no more notice of her blows than of a gnat's sting. Godarz gave ground and parried desperately. As often as not though, a raking claw passed his guard and ripped open his armor to leave a bloody wound.

From the corner of his eye Godarz saw Parysatis rise and stagger toward Tomyris and Xeno, who continued their titanic battle amid the clangor of swords.

Godarz's face was a mask of blood from a slash that would mark him to the end of his days. His chest and arms were raw meat and blood filled his armor and boots. Only a terrible, unnatural vitality kept his battered frame in combat.

The Rakshasa was little better. Time and time again Roxane darted in to strike the demon blows that would have slain a man. Despite the heightened power of the Tokhari and the Amazon, they were not as strong as the heroes of old, and the demon had steeped in his evil and grown in might.

Chandra made his move, darting past the Rakshasa. The demon turned to strike him down and Roxane took advantage to move in and strike a blow. But the Rakshasa had merely feinted, he rounded on Roxane and stuck her a shattering, lethal blow that smashed her to the ground.

TIME SEEMED to slow for Godarz. He saw the cruel gloat in the Rakshasa's eyes. He saw Parysatis strike Xeno from behind, when he flinched Tomyris cut him down. He heard a voice cry out, "Sita!"

The Rakshasa rounded on Chandra in earnest and caught him at the door. The dacoit leader screamed and dropped the jewels he had risked all for. Godarz saw Chandra go down in a wave of blood. Terrible fear and rage swept through Godarz, pinning him to the spot. But the feelings were not his own, with a start he realized he desired nothing. He had a task and he would finish it or it would finish him. For one who was desireless, it mattered not.

Godarz stalked toward the Rakshasa, who had finished disemboweling Chandra. The demon came at him, unstoppable and certain to slay Godarz like a wolf on a rabbit. But a massive ruby, dropped by Chandra, rolled under foot, causing the beast to lose its balance for a moment. Godarz's sword flashed up and struck deep into its foul heart even as the Rakshasa sank its claws and fangs into the Tokhari's sorely mangled flesh.

The Rakshasa writhed and died on Godarz's sword. In agonizing pain, Godarz rose and staggered to Roxane's side. All life was gone, she lay motionless in a pool of blood. Silently, Godarz wept. Tomyris and Parysatis knelt beside him as he clasped Roxane's lifeless hand.

Then a voice spoke. It was a woman and her voice was as beautiful as a mountain stream and as warm as the springtime sun. "Roxane is dead, but Sita has the blessing granted by merciful Parvati. Take it, daughter who carried me, and live."

Roxane gave a great gasp and opened her eyes. "Ohrmuzd, what a dream! I imagined I battled a div from hell with the strength of an ancient queen. But the div slew me and I went before the gods of the Hindus and was restored to life." She sat up and stared wonderingly at her right hand, which she kept tightly clenched.

"Aye, passing strange," Godarz sighed. He looked about the room. It was worse than a slaughterhouse. The dead lay in heaps and blood covered the walls and floor. Where the Rakhsasa had fallen was a mass of putrefied flesh, unrecognizable and horrid.

"At least Xeno didn't get the loot," Tomyris grumbled.

"No, he didn't sister!" Parysatis cried. She was standing at the sarcophagus, the others looked into the crypt that they had risked so much for. It was empty save for rocks and dust.

"Nothing but Illusion. Vasudeva tried to warn me." Godarz learned on his sword wearily. The mighty force that had had given him limitless energy was gone. It had driven him past endurance, like an axe that has hewn wood till its edge is dull and its haft splintered.

Dejectedly, the survivors left the chamber. Somehow Godarz knew the way out, though with every step he felt as if had forgotten part of it. Finally they exited the temple, the sun warmed them and the breeze through the jungle was fresh.

"Well, we gambled and lost," Tomyris said. "Let's ride south. There are plenty of rajahs at war with one another. They'll pay well for our swords, sisters." Tomyris squeezed Parysatis's hand lovingly.

"Our ways part then. I'm for the west," Godarz answered. "I've a mind to see Persia and the kingdoms of the Greeks. I've heard there's a tribe called the Romans. I want to see if they are as mettlesome as men say." He cast a regretful glance at Roxane. "Farewell Amazons. Farewell Roxane."

"You needn't say farewell yet." Roxane smiled. "I will return west too, at least part of the way. I will go back to the steppe country. I'm tired of roving and want to see my kinfolk."

"What then?" Tomyris asked. "Get married to some Saka lout and mind his tent and bear his brats? Then die of boredom?" She snorted in contempt. "Unless a woman is provided for, a man puts a saddle on her and she is but a beast of burden."

"Oh, I'm provided for sister. I have something to get myself firmly in the saddle with something left over for my sword-sisters and Godarz the Demon-slayer." Roxane opened her hand and deftly flipped each of the others a diamond as big as a robin's egg. "A gift from Parvati, or maybe Kali. She's a woman, too, and she knows how to take care of a girl's future."

Godarz held the diamond in his hand and was once again seduced by the shining World of Illusion. ❋

Two Fools for The Price of One

C. J. Burch

Writing about women can be hard work for a writer of the opposite sex. C. J. Burch (who is not a woman hiding behind initials) is one of those rare treasures, a male writer who creates brilliant woman heroes. Whether he's writing about Tiana Dumond and Krystyn Hamerskjold or Narvana Karim and Hana Maleeva in The Star of Kaleel *or any number of other characters, he has that touch that makes his characters sparkle. Reading a C. J. Burch story is to follow exciting people into danger and adventure. This story is no exception. The third Addux and Kouer tale, it is their longest, so far.*

THE BEST swordsmen aren't necessarily strong. They aren't even particularly fast, though speed is more important with a sword than brute strength. Instead, they are cunning. Not in the sense that they understood the writings of the great scholars, but in the sense that they understood themselves. They understand what their body is capable of, what they must do to make it perform at its best. Likewise, they could study and understand an opponent's weaknesses and use them to their advantage.

Addux was such a swordsman. He was of medium height and lean, with brown hair that was turning gray. A well-kept beard covered his pleasant face and his eye like his skin was light. He was not the strongest man she had met, nor was he much in a foot race. He walked with a limp he had earned in the service of the Emperor, and a patch covered his left eye.

Most that met him would have considered him a quiet, courteous man with an easy manner. Until he pulled the sword that hung in the scabbard on his hip. Then he was no longer pleasant or courteous. He was something to be feared.

Kouer wondered at that. Addux was a dangerous man. And he was her man. Years ago, during a part of her life she did not like to recall, she had longed for a simple man with an easy smile and gentle touch. She had told herself she wanted nothing else to do with warriors and their raging tempers. Now she found herself sleeping with another warrior. Her father, just before he sold her into servitude, had observed: "There is something wrong with you."

Perhaps he had been right. Kouer reached out and laid a hand on Addux's shoulder. "You are not well, yet."

Kouer's touch was light as it had always been, and warm. Her voice was pleasant. Addux closed his eyes. And smiled to himself. Then he wondered if dogs and cats derived as much pleasure from the touch of their masters.

"It is time I was out of bed."

"You are not well enough." Kouer shook her head. "You do not remember?"

It was difficult to forget. They had fought a wizard. Addux had lost an eye. Kouer had broken her arm. Kouer's arm had healed. Addux's eye never would. All the same he had grown used to his patch, and the money they had saved had run short.

"Thank you, dearest." He forced himself to smile. "I had nearly forgotten that horror."

Kouer's touch grew less gentle. "That was not the point, man."

Addux knew. Kouer sought to protect him. That was touching, but it wasn't necessary. He turned so that he faced her.

She stood on the other side of their bed. She had changed from her bed clothes into her customary garb. She wore a loose fitting shirt, and a skirt that was slit deeply enough to keep her legs free in a fight, but thick enough to keep her legs warm when the mountain winds blew through the alleys of Azur Kish.

A series of throwing daggers was stuffed into her belt. A leather garrote hung about her right wrist. A heavier dagger, designed for slipping between the cracks of armor, had been strapped to her arm.

"I am sorry, you mean the best for me. Still, I must do something with myself, and if you are going out I might as well follow."

Kouer sighed and shook her head. Her hair, dark as a raven's feathers, fell about her shoulders. "If I wished to be treated as property I would return to my own land."

Kouer was a child of the deserts where women were not allowed to venture beyond their man's reach, even for a moment. She had been cursed with an independent streak that made her life hard, but she was not immune to transparent and obsequious compliments.

"I follow after you because you own me, not because I own you, Kouer," he replied.

Kouer found it hard to reply. When she finally spoke she was hoarse. "Now you are being unfair. Kindness is not permitted in a fight."

That made Addux laugh. "No man alive would fight with you. Crawl before you perhaps, fight with you, never."

Kouer's hoarseness passed. "Now, you are just being obvious."

In truth, he was. Men had fought Kouer, many of them, and they had all regretted the mistake. For though she was not trained with the sword as Addux was she was still dangerous. Those that had once owned her had seen to that.

Their training had made her body as resilient as it was lovely. And though she did not practice her art with the zeal she once had, she still maintained her strength and her agility. In a fight with swords, Addux knew she was not his equal, few were, but without a sword he would not face one such as Kouer. No wise man would.

Addux's smile widened. "I have only begun to be unfair. There are more transparent compliments from whence the last sprang."

Kouer sank to the edge of the bed and lay her forehead against his. "And I want to hear them. I want to hear them for years to come..."

Addux reached out and pulled her close to him. "What a happy coincidence. I want you to hear them."

Kouer laid one hand on Addux's chest and pushed him away gently. Addux as always, appreciated her strength and her beauty, her goose down and her steel.

"If we find work," she said, "you will need to be careful."

"And you won't?"

Kouer shook her head. "Not as careful as you. I am well."

"I promise to be as circumspect as a priest." Addux grinned at her. "Now will you cease your useless worrying."

Kouer shook her head and watched Addux reach for his shirt. "No."

Addux had anticipated that. "If you did, I would be hurt."

WORK FOR Addux and Kouer wasn't something to be

sought. It sought them. That wasn't unusual. Only the youngest of the questionable set they called colleagues actively sought employment. But they had to, they were neither well known nor particularly skilled. Nothing they had done distinguished them from all of the others who hid in the darkest parts of the worst places. They were, quite simply, part of a shadowy gaggle of questionable people looking for questionable jobs. Some of them, if they were lucky and smart would procure a reputation of their own. The rest would die as anonymously as they had lived.

Neither Kouer nor Addux would suffer that fate. Though they were not known to most, each of them was quite famous in the most infamous places, and when they died they would be commented upon at length, if not well. That made Addux smile. "It is good to be among the ones who love us once more."

Kouer surveyed the tavern. It filled a crumbling tower on the northern wall of the old citadel and looked out upon a drop that was beautiful and deadly. A cold wind howled past its windows and forced those seated farthest from its fireplace to snuggle into their cloaks. The sky had turned orange and pink outside and the sun was slipping beneath the horizon. Darkness would be upon the city soon, and would bring with it all the worst perversity man had to offer. About the tavern were seated hard eyed men and dried up women. None of them would have offered Kouer or Addux so much as a kind word if they suddenly burst into flame.

"Yes, the brotherhood of man has always touched me." Kouer signaled the barkeep. He pulled two pints of warmed ale for them and handed them to a serving girl. By the time she arrived at their table, Addux's mood had darkened. Kouer knew him well enough to sense it.

"What's wrong?"

Addux took their drinks and handed the girl a pair of coins. Then he nodded towards the tavern's door. A tall man pulled it closed. He was as thin as famine victim, and his hair and his fingernails were long. He wore a heavy cloak over a robe and carried a gnarled stick. At first glance Kouer wouldn't have thought him a particularly threatening old man, but Addux wouldn't have noticed him if he had simply been an old man. Her eyes narrowed.

"He is an adept?"

The old man turned to face them. Kouer thought his eyes seemed curiously hollow, as if his soul had long ago leaked out of them and left him a shell.

When Addux spoke his voice was not pleasant. "He is not here because he enjoys the company."

That was true enough. Wizards frequented another part of the city. They left it only on business. He was here because he sought someone.

Kouer thought for a moment. "Of course it's us."

Addux said nothing. There was no point. Kouer was right. People in their business met their clients in taverns. Everyone who was anyone one knew who frequented which taverns. Kouer and Addux had long ago staked the *Rampart*. No one else in their line of work had disputed the claim.

The old man searched the tavern silently. When he saw Addux his face was impassive. When he saw Kouer, he smiled. Addux could not blame him for that. Kouer made most men smile. The old man started towards them. Addux signaled the barkeep for another drink.

Kouer frowned. "You know him?"

Addux shook his head. "I've seen his type."

"Where?" Kouer asked.

"In my worst nightmares."

Kouer let that answer be and watched the old man approach. He sat at their table without greeting or introduction. The waitress brought his drink and hurried away.

The old man sipped at his ale and studied Addux for a moment. Finally he nodded as if he were satisfied. Then he turned to Kouer. "Caedyon has disappeared."

Kouer did not know this old man. But of Caedyon she had heard. He was a wizard, supposedly young for his profession and reputed to be both raw and powerful.

"Caedyon and I do not correspond. I do not know here he is."

Addux nodded. "And wizards guard their privacy."

The old man shook his head and reached into his robe slowly, so that he wouldn't alarm Addux or Kouer. When his hand emerged, it held a coin purse.

"There is a small chance that Caedyon might be neither man nor wizard now. If so it will be a time before he can vanish, I think. I want him found." The old man threw the coin purse on the table. Neither Kouer nor Addux reached for it.

Kouer gave the man a smile that could only be called brilliant. "We would rather you open it."

The old man did not seem offended as much as he seemed hurt. "I am so untrustworthy."

Addux shrugged. "We are so cautious."

That stuck the old man as funny. He smiled. "You were not so cautious when last you were in my part of town."

The brawl that had cost Addux his eye had been in the wizards' part of town. He and Kouer took some consolation in knowing the wizard they fought was quite dead. Still, magicians were a clannish lot, oft times given to protecting their own. Thus Kouer and Addux distrusted this one.

Kouer laid one hand on the handle of her dagger. "Open it slowly. I am easily frightened."

Addux agreed. "Believe me there is nothing more terrifying than a hysterical woman with a knife."

The old man opened the purse. Addux saw within it the glint of gold. "Oderkhuul's beard, man. " He pulled the purse from the old man's hand. "Do you want us all killed? You shouldn't be flashing that sort thing in a place like this."

Kouer studied the rest of the clientele. Few of them had bothered to notice the old man or the purse. That was good. The sight of gold had been known to start riots in Azur Kish.

The old man chuckled. "You insisted."

Addux handled the purse the way a king handled his scepter. "If I were a wise man I would still have both my eyes."

"Good," the old man replied. "My name is Meldron. I'm not looking for a wise man. I'm looking for a fool. A hard headed, persistent and dogged fool."

Addux turned a questioning glance upon Kouer. She pried the purse from his hand and peered inside it surreptitiously. After that she smiled.

"You are a lucky man. You've found two fools, and for the price of one it would seem."

ONCE MORE, they stood in the part of Azur Kish reserved for the use of wizards and their servants. Once more, Addux was nervous. His hand did not leave the hilt of his sword. Kouer was not so nervous as her man. She liked the dark. In times past she had done her best work under its cover. Still she was alert. Only a great fool walked into the ward of magicians blithely. Her keen senses detected nothing in the darkness, though, no eyes watched them. No blade threatened them. Addux worried himself for very little reason.

"We could have waited for morning," she said.

Addux grimaced at the thought. Not because he did not like it, but because it was a plan they could follow no more readily than they could leap over the moons above.

"If we come here during the day everyone and their brother's nosy wife will know we search for Caedyon."

Kouer smiled. "I take it few know he is missing."

Not necessarily, just because Kouer and Addux had not heard of the wizard's disappearance did not mean the fact was little known. It just meant that word of his disappearance had not reached their ears before their client hired them.

"We have been out of touch."

Kouer had not thought of that. It made her uncomfortable. In their business knowledge was life. An uninformed slip of the tongue, a poorly planned job...either could be the death of them.

"Surely, we would have heard of Caedyon's disappearance, had it been widely known."

That made Addux smile. He turned to face Kouer. Still his

hand did not leave the hilt of his sword. "We did. The question remains are we one of the first to know or the last?"

Magicians traded in valuable, powerful things. If others knew Caedyon was missing they would be very interested in his house and all that had been stored there. These others would not be so cautious as to let their curiosity go unsatisfied, nor would they be gentle with those who hindered them. Suddenly Kouer's hand moved to the hilt of her dagger.

"I have heard that men should be brawny and silent." Her voice grew anxious.

"My father told me that women were to remain home and raise the children," Addux replied. "We both heard wrong."

Kouer silently cursed herself for her loss of nerve. "I had supposed the danger would not begin in earnest until we found the missing wizard."

Of course, she was wrong. There was no guarantee they were safe now, none at all. Otherwise their client wouldn't have paid them so well. Addux, though, tried not to think of that. He occupied his mind with a question instead. "Where would a wizard disappear too?"

Kouer was willing to play along. "Or if she was taken who would want her?"

"Her?"

"Our client said Caedyon was no longer a man."

Addux thought of the men he had known who were adept in the ways of the arcane. They had all made his skin crawl. "I have known no female wizards. Some say there is no such thing. That there is something in the woman's mind that will not entertain the arcane."

Before them the alley way opened into a broader avenue, a series of stone houses bordered it on both sides. They were an odd mix. Here stood a derelict mansion, there a miserable hovel, beyond that something in between. All of them had this in common, though—they were all in terrible repair.

Kouer surveyed the street silently. "It is said that those who dabble in magic lose interest in the world. That the magics they study and the spells they cast lure them into a realm almost indifferent to our own."

Addux took Kouer's meaning. The houses were ramshackle because those within them cared little for them. "He said Caedyon's house would be here."

Kouer nodded towards a home on the opposite side of the street. It stood near a corner. The plaster that had covered it had cracked revealing the weathered stones beneath. Its windows were dark and the fence about it had crumbled. The massive door that opened onto the street was bronze, but had long ago tarnished and turned greyish green.

Her eyes narrowed. There was a carving on the door. In the gloom one could barely discern it, but it was there all the same, and when the wind blew the clouds apart the moons illuminated it. It was a huge and ornate rune twisted into the shape of a bent "C".

"That's it," Kouer said, "Meldron described the door."

The door was as it had been described. The rest of Caedyon's life, those who might have taken him, even his disappearance was a mystery that had not been explained. Suddenly the gold Addux carried in his pocket did not seem enough. "Let me." He moved in front of Kouer.

Kouer was not so appreciative. "You said you would be careful," she growled at him. "You said you would be as a circumspect as a priest."

Of course that had been a lie. Addux saw no reason to deny it now. "I didn't mean any of that."

He pushed at the door. Its latch, moldered by years of disuse had long since failed. The door fell open. Inside was darkness and dust and the smell of things decayed. Addux felt the hair on the back of his neck stand erect. If he had allowed them his hands would have trembled. "Steady, he whispered to himself. "The house is probably deserted."

Kouer approached his left shoulder. "You think so?"

Once more Addux was brutally honest. "It was a prayer not an assertion."

Kouer wriggled past him and stepped into the room. Once, before the wizards that had owned it had abandoned themselves to the pursuit of ominous things, it had been a sitting room. Beyond it there would be a dining room, beyond that a kitchen... mundane rooms for mundane things. Kouer turned towards the stairs. "If we find anything it will be upstairs, I think."

Addux wondered why. The wizard who had hired them had said Caedyon was missing. That would imply he was not home that he had gone some place else but that led to another question.

"Kouer," he whispered. "Where do wizards go when they go missing?"

Kouer laid a hand on his back and pushed him to the top of the stairs. "That is what we have been hired to find out."

The finding was simpler than Addux could have hoped. At the top of the stairs, a few steps removed from the landing, lying in a beam of moonlight, was a body. Addux nearly smiled with relief. "So that's where they go."

Kouer stepped past him and leaned over the body. It was, or had been, a thin man with unkempt hair and a beard. His robes were old and ill used. His body not so much, though his eyes were sunken and glassy. He seemed young for a wizard.

A few strides closer to the window there was a pentagram. Two of its points had been destroyed and swept away, but the rest remained. Addux did not understand the words scrawled about it, but he didn't suppose he had to.

"He was up to something at the end." Addux stated the obvious. "Has he been dead long?"

With wizards it was hard to tell. They did not bloat and rot like normal creatures. Instead they withered away to ash as if the ties that bound them together had been burned away. Kouer laid a hand on the corpse's shoulder and shook him gently. He was cool, but solid, and not stiff yet, either.

"Not long at all."

Addux thought that odd. "He went missing in his own home for days only to pass recently? That's beyond odd." Still that was a mystery Addux would not waste much time on. For the first time since he had entered the house he almost felt at ease. "But the wizard is found. We have earned our money."

Kouer almost smiled at his optimism. "Not yet. There was something within that pentagram..."

Addux had guessed as much, but they had been hired to locate the wizard, nothing more. "You're not suggesting we look for that?"

Kouer stood slowly. "There is no need to search the city. Still I would look through the house."

That wasn't unreasonable. Addux didn't like it much all the same. He studied the pentagram. "Whatever escaped it killed the wizard?"

That didn't seem likely. There were no marks on the body. "Whatever killed the wizard did him no violence," Kouer replied.

Addux sighed. "Of course I do not understand how wizards live. Why should I understand how they die."

"A wise conjurer does not die." The voice that said it would have terrified an army of well-armed footmen supported by battalions of the heaviest cavalry. "A wise conjurer makes a better bargain."

They turned to find it standing in the doorway of another room. Even in the darkness they could sense it was not human, and it stared upon them with glowing eyes.

Addux drew his sword and stepped in front of Kouer. The monster growled at him and crouched low. Kouer laid a hand on the throwing daggers that hung from her belt. "You have slain the wizard?" she asked.

The crouching thing laughed. Its massive shoulders shook. "Not in the way you suppose."

Kouer wondered at that. Addux did not. What the thing had done with the wizard was completely superfluous. The real question was what the thing was going to do with them... or to them.

"Run," he whispered to Kouer over his shoulder.

"That's funny." Kouer's voice was tight and drawn, like the

string of a bow. "Seriously what would you have me do?"

Addux had expected such a reply, still expecting it did not mean he enjoyed it. "Stay out of the way perhaps?"

The thing before them almost yawned. "You debate a course of action that is worse than useless. I wonder if I was so tiresome?"

Then he gestured towards Addux. There was a low rumble like an escaped cart careening down a hill then something Addux could neither see nor resist slammed into him and drove him backwards. Addux groaned then groaned again when he slammed into a wall. After that he slid to the floor and wheezed weakly.

Kouer cursed herself for allowing Addux out of his bed and leapt towards the creature. It straightened to its full height and reached to intercept her, but it miscalculated her agility and her speed.

Deftly she rolled beneath its grasp and came to her feet driving the heel of her hand into its neck. Her palm met its gray hide with a sold thump. Kouer staggered back a step and reached for her hand instinctively. The impact had nearly shattered it. The creature grinned at her with sharp and deadly teeth and swiped at her with a claw clumsily. Kouer ducked beneath that and forced her sore hand to grab at the dagger in her belt.

The thing advanced upon her awkwardly, as if its skin were a suit it had donned for the first time, and tried to kick her feet from beneath her, but she leapt his attack and drove the dagger into his shoulder with all her strength. There was an ugly snapping noise followed by a metallic ping as the point of the dagger snapped in half. Kouer cursed and tried to retreat. The creature finally snagged a claw in a fold of her shirt and shredded it as it pulled her into its grip, then it drove her against the wall so hard she lost her breath.

As Kouer sank to the floor Addux rallied and charged the beast. It gestured towards him once more and he threw himself to one side. A force he could not see, but sensed all the same, rumbled past him and slammed into the wall where he had fallen. The wall shattered and crumbled into bits. Addux rolled to his feet and charged once more. The creature growled like a saber cat and drove its massive fist into the floor.

The floor buckled and creaked then reeled into the air like a frightened horse. Addux cursed once more and tried to leap through the wreckage but the floor disintegrated about him before he could pull free. Desperately he clutched at the shards of ruined wood that swirled near him, hoping to lay his hands on something substantial and save himself, but there was nothing solid to latch onto, no way to arrest his fall. For a moment there was vertigo, after that there was an impact that shook him to his core and left him alone and cold in the dark.

Kouer managed to roll to her knees as the floor crumbled beneath Addux. By the time she stood most of the room before her had fallen away into the first floor leaving her and the creature standing on a tottering shelf held aloft by buckling wood and what remained of the main staircase.

The creature chuckled darkly and retreated a step through the doorway and into the next room. Kouer howled like a banshee and tore after him. Before the creature could react she was upon him driving a kick into his chest and following that with another. The creature fell back a step and regained its balance. Kouer cursed it for all she was worth and drove a punch into it and followed that with another. The creature hissed at her and reached for her once more but she drew away from it and avoided its grasp.

"You will only make me angry," it warned her.

Kouer did not care. When the floor had fallen away she had felt the best part of her sink away into darkness and nothing. What was left behind was what she had been before she had met Addux, before she had reclaimed her soul. Now she would kill this thing. She would kill it or it would kill her, or if she were truly blessed she would kill it as it slayed her. No matter, there was no use talking, no use wasting time with epithets and oaths. Now there was only death, and death had never cared even a whit for the words and hopes of the living.

Kouer lunged forward and drove a punch into the thing's wide mouth, then ignoring the damage its skin did to her hands, she followed that with another. The creature ignored both punches and tried to tackle her and drive her to the ground. Kouer leapt from his grasp and kicked him in the side of the head so ferociously she feared she had spit her heel in half.

The creature waved towards her and murmured an incantation she did not understand. A stream of flame poured from its hand and screamed towards her. She moved in time but only barely, and the flames screamed past her and into the darkness. The creature cursed. Kouer kicked it again, and again and even once more. It howled in frustration and swept a long looping blow towards her head. She avoided that with ease and stepped close to it so that she could drive more useless punches into its face.

Each punch landed solidly but the creature was not overcome. Instead it weathered the storm and slammed a fist into her side that took her breath away and doubled her over. Before she could recover, the thing drove another blow into the base of her back and sprawled her on the floor. The creature wrapped a paw in her hair and pulled her to her knees. "I told you, you would make me angry." His breath was rancid.

Kouer gasped for air and begged her battered body to leave her be so that she could attack. The creature shook her as if it were a bear playing with its kill. "But you didn't listen, did you?"

It paused as if awaiting a reply. Kouer marshaled what remained of her strength and drove an elbow into its face. The blow surprised the creature but did not hurt it. What followed hurt it though—hurt it a great deal for Kouer drove her fingernails into its eye. The creature howled and tossed her aside before it staggered backwards. Kouer slammed into a wall and sprawled on the floor. By the time she had worked herself to her knees the beast had turned to face her once more.

The creature's right eye shone at her. Its left was mangled.

Bubbling, crimson ocher poured from it. Kouer dragged herself up the side of the wall and forced herself to grin. "I know how to hurt you now," she said raggedly.

The thing roared and made as if to charge her. Then for no reason she could fathom, it hesitated and shuddered. "No," it rasped, "I am in charge here."

Kouer did not know what that meant, nor did she care. She only wanted to hurt it, to kill it. She charged. The thing saw her coming and tried to move aside but she was faster than it was. She slammed into it and bruised her hand upon its tough hide. Then she ripped a throwing dagger from her belt and lunged for its good eye. It jerked its head to one side, and the dagger bounced off its cheek bone. It screamed and slammed a fist into her chest with such force that she tumbled backwards and landed face down on the floor.

Then she tried to push herself to her feet, but it was hard to breathe. She was dazed. The creature fell back a step and gestured towards her. A strange mist rose about her and made her cough. Weakness overtook her and dragged her back towards the floor...

HE HAD thought he was dead, but the pain convinced him otherwise. Death, the legends said was, if not merciful, at least painless. He ached everywhere, ached so viciously it was hard to move. Yet he moved anyway, not because he liked the pain, but because he thought of a woman, a dark haired woman with a brilliant smile and olive skin...

Addux opened his eyes and rolled to one side. All about him was gloom and misery, but he was not alone. There was a voice, a voice very near. It was rough and full of menace and it turned his blood to ice.

"I told you," it said. "I told you that you would make me angry."

Addux pulled himself to his knees and all at once forgot his own misery. Instead he thought only of Kouer. She lay in a heap a half dozen strides from him. To one side of her an old table, worn by time but still solid and strong scuttled about like a crab. Near the table two chairs, whose backs had woven themselves together, danced about strangely. A step beyond the chair a rope slithered across the floor like a python.

Kouer stirred and pushed herself to her feet unsteadily. Addux thought he would throw up. One of her eyes had reddened and swollen, blood trailed from one side of her mouth. Her shirt had been ripped nearly free of her. Bruises too numerous to count covered her and sweat slicked her hair to her head. She struggled to stand and her breath came in ragged gasps.

A few steps beyond her, the creature that had defeated them sat in a comfortable chair. Though one of his eyes was ruined he managed to smile.

"Had enough?" he asked.

Kouer did not waste her strength with a reply. Instead she threw herself towards him, but the chair slid into her path, its legs writhing at her as if it were a hungry ant. She avoided it, just barely, and kicked it aside.

While it fell, the table stood on two legs and lunged towards her. She ducked away from it, but the rope slipped about her legs and she tumbled. She rolled onto her side and came to her knees frantically trying to shake free of the rope, but it slithered up her relentlessly and looped about one of her arms.

With a cry of frustration she managed to stand, but by that time the chair was upon her again. It drove a hard leg into the small of her back and slammed another into her side. Kouer somehow twisted about and kicked it aside.

But as the chair fell the table slammed into her. One stout leg punished her ribs, another her chest. She cried out and staggered. The rope tightened about her and she fell again. The table rained cruel blows upon her.

Addux reached for his sword, but it was not there. His scabbard was empty. The creature in the chair turned towards him and smiled. The table left Kouer be. "You are awake."

Addux did not listen, instead he plotted ways to rend the life from the thing that tormented Kouer with his bare hands. Without much reflection he decided that the easiest path would be the most direct. He leapt for its throat.

The creature gestured at him with a grimace and he slammed into a wall that was clear as a mountain stream and tumbled to the floor. A few strides away, Kouer rolled to her side. She was worn and battered, but all the same she forced herself to smile at him grimly. "I have tried as much," she said weakly, "and met with no more success."

Addux reached for her. The table scuttled between them. Kouer managed to pull herself up on one elbow. "Have I mentioned how happy I am to see you alive."

Addux could manage only a single word, "Kouer."

Again she tried to smile. "I am not so bad as I appear."

The creature nodded and the table smashed a thick leg into her kidneys. She sprawled upon the floor once more. "But," the creature said, "she is not well."

Addux came to his feet, "Leave her be, monster."

The creature shook his head. "No, she has hurt me, hurt me badly. I am entitled to recompense."

Addux crouched low and prepared to throw himself at the thing. It sensed his next move and held up a hand. "But I have need of you which means there is a chance both of you might be spared." Addux listened. He listened because he had no other alternative. The creature grinned. "I need you to slay someone."

Addux had not expected that. "You can't?"

The creature shook with laughter. "Of course, I can. But I cannot do so anonymously...yet. If you can, you will purchase your life, and hers as well."

Addux turned to Kouer. Kouer shook her head. "No," she said quietly, "You will not do this, Addux."

Addux had expected that. The creature had not. It stared upon her. "Suddenly the hellion has scruples?"

Kouer ignored it and turned to Addux. "Not for me."

If the creature did not understand, Addux did. Kouer's past was filled with dark deeds done for dark masters. To this day she struggled with the weight of the things she had done. The death of another who had done her no harm would be more than she could bear. Addux, like all lovers, sought to lighten his mate's load. "Not for you, for me. I place some value on my own life as well."

Kouer knew that to be a lie—not because Addux did not treasure his own life—he certainly did, but he valued hers more. He had from the moment they had met. It was why she needed him so. "Liar," she said.

The creature left that comment be. Instead he concentrated on Addux. "There is a wizard. You will kill him."

Addux silently swore to himself and hoped, should they survive, that he and Kouer would never lay eyes on a wizard again. "Does this wizard have a name. Is there a way he can be found."

"His name is Meldron. His house is not far from here. You can find him if you put your mind to it."

Addux frowned. How would this creature know the man that had hired him? Caedyon and Meldron conspired against it? "You have met this Meldron?"

The creature shrugged. "He would not recognize me. Now off with you. You'll find your sword on the front stoop. I expect you to bring me the head of a wizard before sunrise."

Addux would, or he would die trying. He nodded towards Kouer. "She will be safe when I return."

The creature gave Addux a malevolent smile. "That depends entirely upon her strength and your speed," he replied. "My game shall not cease in your absence, but if you hurry perhaps you will return while she still breathes."

Addux felt his skin redden and ice cold sweat spread across his brow. "I will do this for you." He hoped he did not sound as desperate as he felt. "But if I can kill a wizard, I can kill you."

The creature laughed once more, laughed so hard his shoulders shook and his chins jiggled. "But you haven't killed the wizard yet, have you?"

Addux ground his teeth against one another and controlled

his fear and his hatred if only by inches. Kouer lay where she had fallen on the floor. Though she hated what Addux would do for her, she could not hate Addux. "I have loved you," she whispered.

MELDRON'S HOUSE had not been so hard to find. Neither was it so nice as the home of Caedyon. Of course, that did not necessarily mean Caedyon was the more powerful of the two. Wizards did not purchase their homes. They simply moved into the houses left behind by older wizards whose souls had shriveled to nothing.

Had Kouer been there she would have approached it stealthily, entered it only after observing it for a time. But Kouer was not there, and Addux was missing her presence quite sorely. He decided he would not be subtle. After kicking the front door of the moldering house aside he strode into the center of a decrepit entrance hall. Then he waited. As he expected, Meldron soon appeared.

He stepped out of a shadow into the door way of a connecting room, a puff of smoke and a flash of light accompanied his appearance, more lights shone on his haggard face making him appear stern and mysterious. Addux would have been impressed had he not just faced the monster that had captured Kouer. Compared to that, Meldron now seemed a pathetic imposter, a poseur to be laughed at, but Addux was not there to share a chuckle.

"You asked me to do a job," he said.

Meldron was taken aback, "I told you I would find you," he said.

"So you did," Addux replied, "but things progressed more quickly than I had supposed. I could not wait to report all I have found."

Still the wizard was not at ease. "Where is your woman?"

Addux's eye narrowed. He weighed Meldron's caution against his need to hear what had befallen Caedyon. "Do you wish to hear what I have to say or not."

Meldron's brow wrinkled and he stepped towards Addux. His need to know overcame his fear. "What have you found? Tell me quickly."

Addux did not tell the wizard what he wished to hear, but he did not lie to him either. "I have found that I despise wizards and all their schemes." That said, he stepped forward and drove a vicious punch into the center of the old wizard's face. The wizard fell backwards as if he had been struck by a thunderbolt and toppled to the floor. Addux drove the heel of his boot into the old man's knee with all his strength.

The boot hit home. The old man's leg snapped. He screamed. Addux knelt over him and gripped his wrist then turned it over hard so that the joint nearly gave way. The wizard groaned.

Addux's teeth clenched. Attacking a wizard, any wizard was a hard and dangerous business. They were an oily, tricky lot possessed of great powers. Still they had a weakness. All of their charms required contemplation to cast. If their brains were fogged by terror or pain their magics were not so effective. If he kept Meldron hurt and frightened he could control him, and force him to talk.

"Caedyon," he said, "is dead. The thing that slew him is in his house. It does not seem happy with you."

The wizard gasped. Caedyon's demise did not trouble him so much at that moment. "You have broken my leg."

"And that is not all." Addux was not proud to say it. It was true all the same. "I will kill you if the thing has its way. It seems to hate you a great deal."

"Kill me?" The wizard shook his head as if it made no sense. "Tell me of this thing."

Addux saw no harm in that. "Imagine a creature that could only inhabit your worst nightmare. Then imagine something more loathsome, with thick gray skin and glowing eyes."

The wizard groaned. "The fool said he would call it." Then he frowned. "But why would it slay me. I am not a threat to it. I swear I have not harmed it."

Addux increased the pressure on the wizard's arm. "That is

not what it said. It said it had met you, though you would not remember it."

"Bah. Demons do not appear at the command of mortals. One might hear its voice but meet, it, never," the wizard spat.

Addux frowned. "It fogged your mind with some spell?"

"Will you forget *your* meeting with it?"

Addux could not argue that point. So he seized upon the first explanation that leapt to his mind. "It was in another form?"

The wizard shook his head. "Even if it could take another form I would notice it. Creatures like that are not something a wizard misses."

That made sense. Besides, if the thing could change forms it wouldn't have needed Addux to kill Meldron. Addux frowned. "It lied to me?"

The wizard winced and reached for his trapped wrist with his other hand. "You think that is unheard of? How do you suppose it gathers souls, by telling its victims its true purpose? Tell me what had become of Caedyon?"

"He was dead, though his body was unmarked."

The wizard's dark eyes sparked with an inky light. "Unmarked and fresh as if he had only passed moments before you arrived?"

It was obvious that Meldron knew more than he had told . Addux was displeased. He slapped the wizard's good hand away and wrenched his wrist harder. "It was. Tell me why, tell me why or I will break every bone in your cursed body."

The wizard grimaced. "Because he did it. He accomplished the unthinkable, he mastered that which had mastered him."

Addux did not understand. And he did not have time to reason the matter out. "I am in no mood for subtleties."

The wizard groaned and tried to wriggle away from him. "There is nothing to tell. The creature you faced is of hell itself. It must be stopped. Perhaps if you leave me be I will help you."

The lie was so transparent it made Addux laugh. "Had a street thug told me such a pathetic falsehood I would have killed him for thinking me a fool. You will begin again and this time you will at least approach the truth."

The wizard snarled and turned his dark eyes upon Addux. Addux saw in them a foolish and dangerous thought. He slapped the wizard hard with his free hand. So hard he ruined the wizard's incantation before it was spoken. "So long as I have my hands on you, you are helpless, but I am not. Talk."

With that, the wizard's resistance melted away. "Do you think we are all born with a talent for the arcane? Do you think we drop from our mothers' bodies able to harness the earth's power and turn it to our uses? It is a talent that is purchased."

Addux could guess what would follow. "Purchased from a demon."

That made no sense. "How can you sell your soul more than once?"

The wizard laughed at the warrior's naiveté. "There are the souls of your family, the souls of your friends, the souls of strangers. There are other favors we can give to those we serve as well. There are all manner of things too foul for you to even countenance that we must do. And at the end when it is all finished and we have used ourselves up, there is hell." The wizard shuddered when he said that last and his voice trembled. "There is only hell."

A moment of clear intuition, touched Addux, such as had saved his life in battle many times. He did not doubt it. "Unless one could take control of the demon he served."

The wizard nodded. "If one could surprise him, push him aside and take him, move his soul into its body and move it into his body he could take all his powers as his own."

Addux had not fought a demon. He had fought a wizard that possessed a demon. Still it did not seem possible. "Caedyon's body was dead."

"Not dead - a deep sleep. Caedyon could not allow it to interfere while he grew accustomed to its body. Once he has, Caedyon will awake the demon. In a human body it will be in no position to refuse him. It will be Caedyon's servant. And when Caedyon is finished with it, when he has learned all its secrets and used it up he will shred it and send it to Hell, a faceless, voiceless wreck."

Addux remembered the thing that had attacked him and Kouer. That a man's soul steered it made it more repugnant still. "I didn't realize irony was such a force in the after life."

But Medlorn cared little for Irony. He concentrated instead on Caedyon. "I had thought him mad of course, but when he dropped from circulation I grew curious."

That rang false. "Wizards are not possessed of loyalty and neighborly concern. There is more to your tale."

"You wouldn't be curious?" The wizard riposted. "You wouldn't want to know if he had managed to avoid an eternity in the pit?"

That made Addux smile. "And if he did, how he managed it, eh?"

The wizard sighed painfully. "First I had to know if he lived, or if the demon had torn him to shreds."

That explained how Addux and Kouer had come to their present predicament. It also explained why Caedyon wanted his old drinking companion dead. "The secret of his success is something Caedyon does not wish to share. If you live you might tell of his good fortune. Others would soon try to pry the secret from him."

The wizard laughed at that...laughed almost genuinely. "You have no idea. One of us would soon share Caedyon's good fortune with his own master, then quite literally all of hell would be loosed upon him."

Addux had heard enough of the tale to know what must come next. He would know no more. He was privy to enough misery to drive himself quite mad as it was. He weakened his hold on the wizards arm. "Then as I see it, you have two choices. Aid me in the demons death or die by my hands."

The wizard was unimpressed. "You call those choices?"

Addux smiled grimly. "It is all you have. If I do not kill you, he will send another. If that doesn't work he will eventually come himself."

The wizard could not argue that. "The demon must be destroyed. We shall leave it at that, and hope we succeed."

Addux released his hold. "Then we are allies. Now, tell me how will we do this thing."

KILLING IS not so difficult as it is made out by the holy and wise. Every man, no matter the sanctity of his soul has at one time or another entertained schemes that would make the rest of the world cringe, or at least pretend to cringe. And he does not reserve his most evil plans for the wicked or the truly dangerous. Often as not, his worst dreams, his fondest nightmares involve the blood of those who simply bar him from riches or power. That was why kings had need of royal tasters and dukes had need of their bodyguards.

Few people would admit to this most hard of truths especially about themselves, but it was so. Kouer knew it because she had seen it, and like most who had danced before death's black flame she had learned to be honest, at least with herself.

Still in every killer's career whether he be warrior, or sheriff, thief or king there is a singular moment. A moment when he sees what he doe for the horror that it is and weighs it against the greater good. When he decides whether he can tolerate himself and the blood he has spilled. If he can, he continues apace, content that the carnage behind him will somehow make the future better. If he can't, he does something else.

Her moment had come five years before, back in the east, in the house of a minor potentate with designs on greater power still. She had at the time belonged...belonged? Yes, belonged to a man greater than the minor potentate. This man had bought her as a girl. When it became clear that her strength and temperament would not suit the hall of the concubines he had trained her in her profession.

Said minor potentate had turned his eye towards certain perks that had been reserved to her owner... Even now the memory made her skin crawl, the blood of those she had slain seemed to stick on her hands and face...

"Tell me what you meant." The voice was rough and frightening. The countenance that had birthed it more frightening still. It loomed over her as her head cleared and her senses returned, and stared upon her with a single glowing eye.

"What?" Kouer thought her voice weak. It was.

"You told the man not to slay Meldron, not to slay him for you, why?"

Kouer rolled onto her side. The table and the chairs and the rope had all withdrawn, at least for the moment, though they all hovered about. She imagined they stared at her malevolently, like a pack of wolves waiting for an injured deer to bleed to death.

"I am not worth it."

"You are to the man." The answer had not satisfied her captor.

Strangely, it hadn't satisfied Kouer either. Granted it made sense on its face. But there was something beneath it, something she had not looked at. "He is silly enough to love me."

The demon hesitated. Turned its head so that its remaining eye focused upon her more clearly. "Not so silly. Now tell me the truth."

Kouer pushed herself to her knees and wrapped her arms about herself as if that would hide her from the demons gaze. His undivided attention made the tables and the chairs seem pleasant by comparison.

"Demons seek the truth?"

A low rumbling laugh quivered in the demon's chest. Suddenly it bared its fangs at her. Its voice grew deeper, more savage. "Seek it? No, but we all find it, whether we wish to or not. For most, it is the final tragedy in a miserable life."

Kouer's eyebrows arched. Her attention, which had been focused on her own misery suddenly shifted. "And now, I find demons are wise as well. It has been a strange evening."

The demon leaned towards her. "We are more than trash like you will ever understand. Only the gods..."

It had begun rather like a tale told by a bard. With a spirited opening that was sure to lead to a lengthy dissertation. But as quickly as it had begun, it ended. The demon's expression changed and his voice died. He rocked backwards and gurgled, then as suddenly as the fit had come, it was gone. The demon steadied himself and eyed her again.

"Tell me." When he spoke once more his voice was different...more desperate. "Tell me why you are not worthy. Tell me...tell me now."

Kouer did not oblige. "Why must you know? I have never heard that demons were selective as to the content of the souls they collected."

The demon grimaced, but for some reason the expression was not so horrible now. Compared to the look it had given her moments before it seemed almost childish. "I do not have to explain myself to you or to anyone else now." The table scuttled forward and slammed a leg into the middle of Kouer's back. She toppled forward "Tell me or I will loose them upon you again."

Kouer rolled onto her back and cataloged her hurts. They were many and serious. Worse, she was tired, tired beyond words. She no longer had the strength or will to fight with the demon's toys. If he loosed them upon her again they would pound her into jam.

"My past has not been exemplary."

The demon shuddered once more, its shoulders shook and a bit of drool rolled out of the corner of its mouth. "Yes." The voice was deep again, self-assured and terrifying. "I smelled it on you when you first stepped into my view. How many have you killed? Can you remember them all? Do you wish to?"

In truth, she did not wish to, but she did. She remembered them all. Sometimes late at night they visited her, and made her very grateful that Addux was there to wrap about her. She closed her eyes. "I have no choice."

"And they trouble you?" the demon asked.

Kouer smiled. "Apparently, I am reprehensible enough to commit the foulest of deeds but not so reprehensible as to enjoy them."

The demon's laugh was harsh. It hurt her ears. "Of course, most of you tend in that direction. It is a weakness. It takes a certain amount of courage to enjoy the worst parts of oneself, you know. No matter." He leaned closer to her. "Courage like anything else can be learned with the proper incentive and discipline. Given time your past will not trouble you."

"What?" Kouer wondered if the pounding she had taken had shaken something loose in her skull.

"It is very simple, woman. I am important. I always have need of servants. Based entirely upon the damage you have done to me I think you qualify."

Of course that made no sense at all. "Then why did you bargain with Addux?"

The demon grimaced. "Who says I did? Besides, the man is another fool with a sword. They are beyond disposable, useful only on battlefields. You are a much more flexible asset, with many more uses. All you need is a will to live."

A will to live? She had heard that before. Of course the language had been different, the phrasing not so exact, but the meaning had been the same. Her last owner had said it. He had said it when she began her service with him. The understanding had been simple. So long as she discreetly killed those he wished dead he would treat her as a loyal and valuable pet. Should she ever fail...should she ever refuse her services then she would not be so valuable or so useful.

Strange, at the time the bargain had not seemed so vicious. She lived as well as one of her birth could hope and those that died upon her blade could never be confused with saints. If she was not one of the good she was at least one of the necessary. And she always seemed to slay those who had worked to deserve the death she bestowed upon them.

But life, inconvenient thing that it is, has a way of destroying illusions. Her own had died in the house of the minor potentate who troubled her owner. In the end she had killed him in his own bed while he slept. Had she not been discovered by his son...had his son not tried to avenge his father. She could not pretend the boy's death had been deserved, and that had made all the difference, then and now.

Kouer was no saint. She feared death and the judgment that would assuredly follow more than most, with good reason. Still, she could not serve this demon, for if she did somewhere along the line she would run across another boy whose only sin was defending his father. She slowly pushed herself to her feet.

"No."

She had expected the demon to condemn her with indignant outrage. Instead he shuddered and his misshapen face turned venal and petty. "See?" He hissed in a high pitched voice. "I was right. I was right again."

Right about what? Who was the demon speaking to? What the bloody hell was he talking about? All questions that went unanswered, for a moment later the table fell upon her. She sensed its movement and sidestepped it, but the chair followed on its heels. She blocked its attack with her forearm and earned herself another bruise before she kicked it over, but the rope looped about her ankles before she could turn towards the table and she fell to the floor After that the table kicked her in the back so heavily it took her breath away. The chair righted itself and slammed a blow into her aching ribs . She thought she might pass out, but she did not.

The furniture ceased its attack and the rope tightened its grip on her legs. When her head cleared she found the demon staring down at her.

"Nonsense." His voice was deep and threatening again. "All the spirited mounts buck a bit in the beginning. She will serve. Watch me work."

For the life of her Kouer could not understand what the demon meant. "What are you talking about? What is wrong with you?"

The demon shuddered more violently than he had before . "I will not watch you. I am master now. I will decide what is to come next. Only me."

"Only you?" The demon replied. "Hardly. You and all like

you are built for the short haul. A blink in time exhausts your possibilities. I will bend you to my will as easily as I did before."

While the demon formulated a reply to its own taunt, Kouer rolled onto her back and desperately fought the living rope that bound her. The most sacrilegious of the philosophers had long ago scraped together the temerity to claim that the gods were insane.

They had posited, before they were hunted down, arrested, tried as heretics and burned alive, that one only need look at the state of the world to see that the powers that ran it had long ago lost their bearings. If the demon was any indication, the priests that lit the flames about those long dead philosophers' feet owed them an abject and unreserved apology...

ADDUX'S PATIENCE with the wizard, which had not been of an unlimited supply even in the beginning, had worn away to nothing. "You are slow."

"You broke my leg." The wizard did not think Addux's point foolproof.

That memory, even in these most desperate of times, made Addux smile. "You say it as if I have done a bad thing."

Of course the wizard believed he had. Addux did not care much about the ethical implications of the act. It had certainly felt good. For now that was enough for him. Besides they had arrived. Caedyon's house was at the other end of the block. Its massive door was still ajar. Inside was the wreck the demon had created when he collapsed the landing beneath Addux. Of course Kouer was inside as well. Addux prayed she had fared better than the staircase.

Addux started towards the house. "Here."

The wizard nodded. "I know Caedyon's house."

"A pity you didn't investigate his disappearance yourself."

The wizard smiled at Addux's reply. "He would have killed me."

So he would have, but that was nothing to Addux now. So long as Kouer was inside of that house and in trouble, little else mattered. He slipped an arm about the wizard's bony shoulders and dragged him forward. "You are certain this will work?"

The wizard gave him a look that would have frozen lesser men to death. "Of course, I kill demons all the time. Slayed two before breakfast this morning and a third while I was preparing my dinner. No, I have no idea whether this will work or not, you imbecile." The wizard reached into his robe and fingered the bottle he had shown Addux earlier.

In truth he suspected the concoction he had prepared would work. If anything could tear the body of a demon apart it was this. Of course, he hadn't prepared it for this exact eventuality. Still, if it worked and this turned out fairly well, he would be a very lucky man, indeed.

"I wonder how I shall adjust to that?" He hadn't realized he had said it aloud.

"Adjust to what? " Addux dragged the wizard forward at a break neck pace.

The wizard avoided the question. "It will hear you."

At that, Addux returned to his work dragging the wizard through the ruined house silently. The wizard winced as they stumbled over a bit of broken masonry that clogged the old house's doorway. Then he dropped his staff. "Wait."

Addux did not pause. "There is no time."

"I cannot walk without it."

Addux did not relent. "If we succeed you can retrieve it. If we don't, you will never need it again."

The wizard did not bother to argue. There was no point. Addux's statement had been of ironclad truth. Instead, he whispered a final instruction. "Get me close to him. Get me close to him and keep him busy."

Addux paused at the base of the ruined stars. Above them in the darkness he could hear the demon's guttural voice . Another voice replied. Higher pitched and more irritating, but similar. The demon was arguing with someone. With someone that was not Kouer.

He pulled the wizard onto his back and charged up the

ragged steps. "If you fail and the demon does not slay you, I will."

Of course, that was not an idle threat, but it was useless all the same. "If I fail, the demon will chew our skins off and watch what is left flop on the floor before him like a scaled fish."

"Then if you fail, I will slay only myself and leave you alive," Addux replied.

The wizard gave him a hollow grin. "But you are a vicious bastard."

KOUER HAD discovered long ago that all men, whether they wished to believe it or not, truly were the sum of other's perceptions. Rulers who commanded great armies and navies could still be pathetic weaklings if in the eyes of their subjects they appeared uncertain or frightened. Likewise, petty thieves of no particular distinction and with no outstanding prospects could still be brave and fine men so long as the people that surrounded them thought them so. Simply put: a reputation could build a man as easily as a man could build a reputation. And once that reputation was built, it was nearly impossible to change. People simply would not tolerate the change. Knowing that now, Kouer could not help but look upon the demon who had frightened her and tormented her with something almost akin to pity. Akin to pity, but not outright pity.

The argument it had started with itself had continued even as she fought the rope that bound her legs, growing more shrill and more obscene as it progressed. And now as she finally unwrapped the last of the rope from her ankles, the demon was arguing with itself in two voices, one a rugged bass and the other breathless tenor. Each voice in the course of the argument had increasingly eschewed wit for obscenity as time had passed and now seemed to be howling incoherent curses at one another.

And as powerful as the demon was, as much as she should fear it, she did not, not any more. For no matter its strength in the end, it was still an addled and sad creature incapable of governing even its own thoughts. That did not make it less dangerous of course, but its danger did not make it less sad either. And had Kouer not been so intent upon escape she would have paused to ask it: "Have you no pride at all?"

But she was intent on escape therefore she kept her questions to herself and toiled at the rope. The demon paid her little mind. Instead, it staggered to one side and shuddered more violently than it had before. Then it screamed an insult at itself that would have inspired any man its subject to challenge the demon to a duel.

The table and the chairs though were not so preoccupied as their master. They moved towards her. Kouer cursed and sidestepped the chair then kicked it aside. But the table was too fast. It charged into her before she could react and drove its leg into her stomach. She groaned as the air left her and collapsed on her side. Her ribs, all ready battered, complained at her horribly. Kouer rolled onto her side and gasped. Her vision faded.

Then Addux appeared at the top of the stairs carrying a skinny and decrepit old man with a flowing beard and an injured leg. It was the wizard who had hired them at the beginning of this disaster. Before she passed out, Kouer could not help but think he would have been better served had he carried his sword instead.

BY THE time Addux cleared the top of the steps his lungs and his back were straining under the extra weight of the wizard, but the sight of Kouer unconscious at the demon's feet made his misery seem far less.

"Do your job, wizard." He tossed the old man aside and raced towards Kouer.

The wizard landed hard and wrapped himself around the bottle he had brought from his home so that it would not break upon the floor.

"Fool!" he howled at Addux. "I must be nearer the demon."

Addux did not hear him. His mind was focused entirely upon the woman that lay at the demon's feet. When he neared the demon he drew his sword. The demon paid the blade no mind. Instead, it looked upon the hobbled wizard.

The creature said in the strange high-pitched voice Addux had heard before, "You have come to visit."

Addux thrust his blade towards the demon but the table and chair that had tormented Kouer interceded. The table parried Addux's strike with a leg. The chair leapt towards him.

Addux kicked the chair away and tried to shoulder the table aside. It backed away from him awkwardly and prepared to strike again. A few paces away, the wizard finally managed to come to his feet painfully. He studied the demon's hulking body as he limped forward. "So, that is what it looks like," he muttered more to himself than anyone else. "I had only heard the voice."

The demon's shoulders hunched and its expression changed. It was something different from what it had been before. "Another of my gnats appears. This is what I look like, dog." Its voice was deep now as deep as it had been when Addux first happened upon it. "Fall on your face before me."

That took the wizard back. "What?" He nearly forgot the bottle he carried in his right hand. "What did you say?"

The demon stepped away from the furniture that sparred with Addux. "You heard me, dog. Did you think I would not recognize you? Your soul is like the back of my hand."

Addux ducked away from a table leg and kicked the chair so hard he nearly snapped it in half. The table advanced upon him again. He called to the wizard. "Do it, old man. Do it now."

The demon laughed. "This dog can't do anything, not without my approval. I own him."

Addux had not expected that. He slammed the pommel of his sword into the table and drove it away from him so that he could turn unmolested. Then he looked upon the wizard once more. The old man was bewildered. Addux, who had been desperate before, was suddenly frightened beyond reason. Not knowing what else to do, he stated the obvious. "It will kill us."

The wizard blinked. When he spoke, his voice was unsteady. "But this is wrong. Caedyon didn't succeed. Can't you see he didn't succeed."

At the sound of the name, a tremor ran through the demon. The expression on its face was not so frightening as before. "I am here." The voice was high pitched again, high pitched and frightened, as if it struggled against a wave of irresistible panic. "I am here. But it is hard. It is hard. You must help me. If you help me, then I can help you."

Addux was hopelessly confused. If Caedyon had not succeeded, what was wrong with the demon? What was it talking about? The table and the chair did not allow him to ponder the questions. One drove a leg into his shoulder, the other rapped him across the knees hard. Addux cursed and staggered backwards. The table slammed into him and he toppled.

As he fell the wizard shook himself free of his trance and slid forward once more. "I rather thought—" His voice was steadier now. "—that one way or t'other there would only be one of you in there."

The demon laughed oddly. "We seem to be sharing accommodations."

"Not for long." The demon's affect and voice changed. The frightened quality was replaced by grim certainty. "He will not stand against me. Little by little I push him aside. Soon he will be nothing." Then his affect changed again, and the demon, for all his monstrous strength, seemed a frightened child. "Not nothing. I will never be nothing— I am Caedyon."

Another tremor shook the demon, and his voice was a low rumble. "It is inevitable, one such as he is only an annoyance, but a time consuming annoyance all the same. There are certain rites you could perform, rites that would help me subdue him. I will reward you quite handsomely."

On the floor, Addux struggled against the table and the chair. Their legs pounded at him ceaselessly. "Wizard." He almost pleaded.

The wizard inched forward, ever forward. "I believe Caedyon was making an offer before you interrupted."

The demon's good eye twitched nervously, but his voice remained steady. "From him you will never collect. This is a battle I will win in the end. I only ask you to shorten it. You will not enjoy my wrath if you refuse me."

The wizard cocked an eyebrow as if contemplating a reply, but the demon's visage changed once more and the voice of Caedyon called to him. "Do not listen to him! We can overcome him. We can defeat him."

The wizard sighed and dragged himself one step closer to the demon. "But you sent the warrior to kill me."

"A mistake. I see your value now."

"Always we see the value in things when it is too late." The wizard crammed a lifetime of regret into that statement. He leaned forward and threw the bottle toward the demon with all his strength. The bottle shattered when it struck him. A shimmering liquid spread over him and hissed, then the demon turned white hot and began to dissolve like a cube of sugar thrown into a cup of tea. The wizard tried to retreat but the demon howled, not in Caedyon's voice but in his own. Apparently it had decided it would die a demon. It had also decided it would not die alone. "Come here, fool," it growled at the wizard. "I will escort two souls into the void this day."

The wizard gasped and tired to run but his shattered leg folded beneath him and he fell. The demon took a faltering step forward and fell upon him. Then there was a great and smoky hiss and a burst of heat so strong Addux feared it had singed away his hair. After that there was silence. The table and the chair both left him be and collapsed to the floor uselessly and lay near the body of Caedyon.

Addux sat up slowly and crawled to Kouer. She breathed sill. He laid a hand in her hair and her eyes fluttered. "Rest," he said.

Kouer swallowed hard and emerged from a nightmare world composed of shadow and dream. "I thought I heard the demon."

Addux turned to the great greasy spot where the demon had been. "He will speak no more."

Kouer sat up slowly and resisted the urge to sob. "And the wizard?"

"Gone with the demon."

Kouer nodded and leaned against Addux's chest. Then she wrapped her arms about his neck. "At least he paid us."

Addux laughed gently and cradled Kouer against him. "For that I will try to remember him well. I will find you a healer."

Kouer shook her head. "No. I will not be prodded and bothered by one I do not know or like. Help me up. Take me home."

Without another word Addux wrapped his arms about Kouer and lifted her from the floor. Then Caedyon sat up as if he had started from a nightmare. Addux stood dumbfounded. Kouer wriggled from his arms, brought her feet to the floor gingerly and leaned against him. "Should I have expected this?" was all she could think to say.

Addux disposed of his wonderment and reached for his sword. "A sterling explanation is in order Caedyon."

The wizard shook his head. His voice was unsteady. "I am Meldron. Can't you see I am Meldron?"

Kouer chose to be obvious. "No."

The wizard made a feverish effort to explain. "After the darkness, after the great burning steam there were three of us. The demon and Caedyon struggled with each other as they fell away. They were so intent upon one other they did not notice me. I reached for the open spot left behind, for the single sliver of light above us. Somehow I anchored myself." He paused trying to comprehend it all. "They were sucked away."

Kouer frowned, "The wizard who hired us, has taken the body of the wizard who died."

"The wizard who took the demon," Addux corrected her. Kouer frowned at him quizzically. "There will be time for explanations later." He drew his sword. "It would seem a neat plan, wizard."

"No." Meldron turned to him frantically, "Leave me be. Do not hurt me again." Then he hissed a quick incantation...

And nothing happened, nothing at all. The night remained as still as a tomb. Addux added what the wizard had told him to what he had seen, and laughed. "No wonder the demon recognized you. You were his, as well."

The wizard closed his eyes. "I was.. In a pinch one always returns to his old habits, even when they are useless." He paused and his eyes moved from Addux's sword to the warrior's face. "It was all happenstance. Caedyon was a stubborn fool. I held out no hope for his success. Whether he rode upon a stroke of brilliance at the end or pure luck I will never know. But once he had started this foolishness, what else could I do. What else would you have had me do? Besides, what more can you do to me? I am free but I am nothing, nothing. Had I known it would come to this I would have tried harder to convince Caedyon to leave this foolishness be."

Addux put away his sword. He had seen soldiers given second chances. Men who had somehow survived horrific wounds and terrible odds. Some of them, a few, actually became good men because of the experience. It was as if seeing death pass so close, yet not touch them had convinced them that there was a purpose for their lives. Would such happen to the wizard? Probably not. But there was a chance. And Addux, though no gambler, was never one to automatically dismiss long odds out of hand.

"Actually wizard you are more valuable than a free man."

The wizard stared at him with tiny, panicked eyes. "I thought it would be wonderful, but now I am alone, powerless and penniless. What value could I possibly have?"

Addux slipped an arm about Kouer and gently turned her towards the door of the ruined house. "You are a man who might make himself noble one day," he replied.

Kouer could not leave that be. "If you live and if you can stand the pain." ✽

Pieces In A Game

Jack Mackenzie

The hardest thing is to write about yourself in the third person. The second hardest thing is to write about someone you've known almost your whole life. You remember when you used to share Edgar Rice Burroughs novels, read Conan comics, saw all the Star Wars *films together and even began to attempt the writing of stories and the creation of artwork. Jack Mackenzie, who goes by another name during daylight hours, has been creating Fantasy tales for many years now. I've been lucky enough to read just about all of them too. "The Pieces in a Game" is his longest story in the Sirtago and Poet series, a buddy series of sorts. I have to wonder if he based them on us and if so, which one am I?*

1. RAMEL

THE DESERT heat made the air shimmer and dance and it wrapped around Poet like an unwelcome blanket. He peered around the rock behind which he was crouching to get a better look at the intruders.

There were three of them riding camels, moving cautiously through the gap that formed the only approach to the Kajaghn's encampment. They held lances and Poet could see swords and daggers amongst their equipment. He could also see fat packs loaded with provisions.

He glanced at Sirtago who had his sword ready. He was crouched behind an outcropping some feet away and doing a poor job of it. Poet could see him squirming and shifting, as if trying to scratch an itch. Poet knew his old friend well enough to know that this particular itch could only be scratched with spilled blood.

Poet could only see Sirtago in profile. The scarred side of his face, the side that was missing an eye and which sported the twisted tooth that grew from between his lips like a tusk, was facing away from Poet. From this vantage Sirtago looked like a normal man — was even handsome in his way — but Poet could see clearly the boy that Sirtago used to be, Poet's childhood companion and protector. He could see Sirtago's familiar childish impatience working in him even now.

The intruders were now at the encampment. They stopped and stared at the abandoned camp with puzzlement and apprehension. Suddenly the air was split with a high whistle. It was Ussan's signal. Poet leaped from behind his rock and drew his daggers. Poet saw Sirtago bolt from his hiding spot like a hound after a rabbit.

The surrounding hills were now alive with Kajaghn fighters, pouring down towards the intruders. Ussan himself was in front, his weapon drawn and steady.

The largest of the intruders leaped from the back of his camel and drew a large curved blade. The other two remained on their mounts.

Poet saw Ussan slow and stop. He saw his stance relax. Ussan threw back his head and the small canyon that the Kajaghn called their home rang with his laughter.

Poet relaxed. The intruders were known to Ussan, that was clear. Then Poet saw Sirtago, still advancing, his weapon raised to strike.

"SIRTAGO, NO!" Poet shouted. His voice echoed off the rocks. Ussan turned and flicked up his sword, stopping Sirtago's downward stroke in time to prevent it from disembowling the newcomer. The swords clashed and the ringing echo died away.

Ussan turned to the Kajaghn. "These are friends!" he said. "This is Lan. He is a guard from my palace and a trusted servant."

"Then why did they sneak up on us?" Sirtago growled, his anger still smouldering.

Ussan turned to Sirtago and gave him a hard look. Poet marvelled that Ussan could look directly upon Sirtago's frightening visage and not turn away in disgust or fright. "Sheathe your anger along with your sword, Sirtago. These are friends"

Ussan turned away from Sirtago and embraced his friend.

Poet found his way carefully down the rocky slope towards the newcomers. The Kajaghn surrounded them, all curious about their identities.

The middle rider had dismounted now and Poet could see that he was a boy. He was of the age of manhood, but barely. The boy approched Ussan. "How goes it with you, my brother?" the boy asked.

Poet saw a look of disapproval cloud Ussan's features. "What are you doing here, Ramel?"

"I have come to join the war. I want to fight the Tey'ei."

Ussan let out a noise of displeasure. "I see," he said. "And does Father know you are here?"

"Of course he does," Ramel said. Poet saw Ussan's eyes flick upwards to the one newcomer who was still mounted, an older man. The man shook his head at Ussan.

Ussan returned his gaze to his younger brother. "No lies, Ramel! You shame me with them."

Ramel became upset at the rebuke. "I want to join the war!" he protested. "I want to be part of the holy campaign against the Tey'ei."

Ussan shook his head. "I am most displeased, Ramel. But we will speak of this later." Ussan moved to the older man and helped him dismount. "Zushan," he said, and embraced the elder man warmly.

Ussan turned to the Kajaghn fighters. "We will celebrate tonight — a feast in honour of our guests!"

The collective cheer from the Kajaghn rang throughout the canyon.

USSAN'S TENT was full that night. His lieutenants and his closest friends and advisors sat close to him and his brother and retainers. Sirtago and Poet sat inside the tent as well. They lie on cusions and ate and drank and enjoyed the merriment.

Ussan and his brother talked in low voices. Poet could not make out what they were saying but they seemed to be having a disagreement. It was clear that Ussan Cho Kassen, leader of the Kajaghn fighters, prince of the house of Eidos, did not want his young brother Ramel to be mixed up in the dirty business of fighting the Tey'ei.

For that matter, Poet did not want to be mixed up in it either, but here he was. They had left Trigassa to join the holy cause six months ago. The invasion of Natsa'ug by the Tey'ei Vaus was well known even in southern kingdoms like Trigassa. It was known that rebels had formed an army to repel the invaders and that its leader was a prince of the Ibarra Eidos.

Sirtago was a fervent follower of Ussan Cho Kassen now, but not because of the Tey'ei, or even because of the opportunities for loot and pillage that came his way. Only Poet knew Sirtago's real reason for being here.

Poet felt a soft hand on his shoulder. Kiessy's lust-filled eyes and sweet, full lips smiled at him, inviting him to come. Poet smiled back and nodded and Kiessy withdrew.

Sirtago was busily arguing sword techniques with two Kajaghn. No one was paying any attention to Poet. All eyes were on their leader and his conflict with his brother.

He took note that Agon, Ussan's chief lieutenant, was sitting near Ussan, attentive to him. Poet slipped off of his cushion and made his way out of the tent.

Outside the Kajaghn were celebrating with drink and crude songs. They surrounded Ussan's tent in noisy crowds. Poet made his way through them, out towards the main camp and to his tent. To anyone observing him, he was merely another soldier trying to find a place to relieve himself.

By the time he got to the edge of the encampment Poet was alone. He found his tent. He could hear Kiessy moving around inside. He climbed in and her soft laughter provoked his manhood to ready itself.

She grabbed at his clothes, tearing and pulling until all was free. Poet similarly liberated her and they began a wild, frenzied passion dance that had become familiar to both of them.

POET WAS dozing in the warm afterglow, his head resting on Kiessy's soft parts when he heard a noise that brought him fully back to wakefulness. It was the sound of ripping cloth. Poet opened one eye and saw the tip of a blade piercing the side of his tent.

Poet rolled out of the way on top of Kiessy narrowly missing the downward thrust of a sword.

"Oh, lover..." Kiessy began, giggling back into wakefulness, and entwining Poet in her arms. The blade withdrew and a pair of hands reached in through the tear and pulled.

The side of the tent was ripped wide to reveal Agon holding his sword for another thrust, a wild fury in his eyes.

"Dog!" Agon shouted. Poet scrambled out of the way as the

blade came down again, narrowly missing both of the lovers. Poet got to his feet, grabbing at his shirt as he did.

Kiessy tried to get up. "Husband, no," she said, frantically. "It's not what you think. He attacked me! He's a raving beast!" He..."

Agon struck Kiessy with the back of his hand. "Silence, Whore!" he shouted. Kiessy tumbled into the remains of Poet's tent.

Agon turned his fury back towards Poet who tried feebly to cover himself with his shirt. "Die, you rutting swine!" Agon shouted and swung his blade at Poet.

Poet closed his eyes for the blow, but it never came. Instead the clash of steel on steel rang in his ears. He opened his eyes to see Sirtago, his blade out, his ruined face contorted in an angry yell.

Poet dropped to his knees and scrambled out of the way as Sirtago and Ussan's Lieutenant fought amongst the ruins of Poet's tent.

Poet managed to put on his shirt and find his trousers when Ussan arrived with a crowd of Kajaghn behind him.

"What is the meaning of this?" Ussan demanded. He drew his blade. "Agon! Sirtago! Put up your swords!"

Agon did as he was bid by his leader, the fury still smouldering in his eyes. Sirtago took advantage and moved in to strike a fatal blow. Ussan darted forward, his blade flashed and Sirtago's weapon went flying into the night air.

"I SAID STOP!" Ussan bellowed at Sirtago. Poet could see Sirtago's rage boiling inside of him, but reason soon calmed him. He stood quietly, but his hands opened and closed reflexively.

"My husband..." Kiessy's muffled voice broke into the tense silence. All eyes were drawn to the shape that moved amongst the torn tent. Ussen stopped, reached in and pulled Kiessy to her feet. Her body was wracked with sobs, her cheeks stained with tears. She shook her head, her eyes pleading at Agon. "Husband, hear me... It was not I who was... It was him... He overpowered me..."

The surrounding Kajaghn collectively stifled outbursts of mirth at this feeble protest. Kiessy was a tall woman and, though voloptuous, was solidly built and strong. Poet was a foot shorter and slight of frame. The Kajaghn had a difficult time imagining Poet's supposed ability to overpower Agon's wife.

"You lying slut...!" Agon began, but was silenced by a look from Ussan.

USSAN SAT on a cushion in his tent. Poet was now dressed, though he felt rumpled and askew. Kiessy was also covered now and her tears and protestations were replaced by a sour expression.

Ussan glared at Poet. He glared at Kiessy. He glared at Agon and at Sirtago. "This situation is intolerable." he said quietly. "We are an army with a holy cause. I cannot have this kind of disruption in the ranks."

Agon bowed his head. "I will leave, then, Master," he said, contritely. "I will take my wife and we will return to our village in Kastan..."

Ussan shook his head fircely. "That will *not* do. I need you beside me more than ever now. Your wife will return to your village. She will go east to Kastan with Lan, my trusted guard and Zushan, my old retainer. Her virtue — what is left of it — will be safeguarded until she is returned to her mother's house."

Agon nodded once. Kiessy's eyes burned with outrage but she remained silent. Ussan turned to Poet.

"As for you," he said. "Your continued presence here would be disruptive. Agon is not a man who forgives easily, and he never forgets. However, your service is valuable to me and I am loath to dismiss you out of hand. Therefore I will charge you to return my young brother Ramel safely back to his home in the Ibarra Eidos."

Poet felt suddenly dizzy. It was a long a treacherous journey through the western lands. He would be responsible for keeping the youth safe from harm. Failure in this regard would surely mean his death.

"You can't send him alone!" Sirtago spoke up.

"Do you have so little regard for your friend's ability?" Ussan asked.

"No! It's just... He's only one man. He should have an armed escort."

Ussan smiled and Poet suddenly realised that Sirtago had fallen into the warlord's well baited trap. "Since you are so concerned about your friend's safety, then I will send you with him as a guard against the dangers of the way."

Sirtago's mouth opened in shock. "I didn't mean me!" he protested. "I meant someone else!" Sirtago shook his head in frustration. "What about the Tey'ei enclave? We were going to strike..."

"An action that we will have to carry out without your presence, Ka Sirtago," Ussan said smoothly. "You must understand that the safety of my younger brother is paramount. You will accompany Poet back to Ibarra."

THE SUN rose slowly over the Nats'n's western desert. Poet, Ramel and Sirtago rode in silence. Sirtago had fumed and stormed his way through the pre-dawn departure preparations. Poet knew better than to try to engage him in any conversation. It was best to let him huff and curse on his own until his anger was spent.

Ramel had enjoyed the previous night's celebrations overmuch and was suffering because of it. The bright sunrise was now illiciting a fresh stream of moaning from the youngster, who slumped forward on his camel.

Poet alone was content. He had joined Ussan Cho Kassen's holy endeavour along with Sirtago, not out of any abject hatred of the Tey'ei, but because Sirtago needed to leave his home in Trigassa.

Sirtago's reasons had nothing to do with the political situation in the Nats'n, nor with any religious reasons. Sirtago couldn't give a toss about the Nats'n's angry gods or their outrage at the practices of the Tey'ei. Sirtago's reasons for joining the Kajaghn fighters was purely personal and Poet knew it full well, but never dared speak of it with him.

Now he was leaving the desert lands and returning to civilization. The Eidoss was a rich kingdom with many earthly pleasures. There was art and music and food and women. Ramel was the youngest of the Cho Kassen family and they were very wealthy. They were not Ootin merchants, but they provided services for them, and the Ootin merchants were wealthy beyond the imagination.

Poet let his thoughts drift to the heady aroma of spices and sweet smoke. He thought of cushions and blankets and beds with real sheets spun from the threads of worms. He was content to leave behind the dust, the cold nights and the acrid smoke of watch fires — of badly cooked meat and hard bread.

He thought of paper for writing and verses he could compose.

And, though he tried not to, he thought of Jeswana, home and safe in Trigassa, and of his own broken heart.

The sun was fully overhead and the heat of the day rose about them. Poet looked forward to the cooler climes of the Eidoss and plentiful water.

Ramel had perked up a bit since the morning. He became more gregarious as the day wore on. He was unused to spirits, particularly the potent swill that was favoured by the Kajaghn, but he was young and strong and had recovered well enough.

"Did you see many battles?' Ramel asked him. "Have you killed many Tey'ei?"

Poet shrugged. "I have killed my share. Ka Sirtago has killed his share as well, and twice more that number."

Ramel regarded Sirtago riding ahead of them with a look of curiosity. "What happened to Sirtago's face?" Ramel asked in a whisper. "Was he captured by Tey'ei and tortured?"

Poet smiled. "No. Nothing so romantic. He has been like that since birth."

Ramel looked at Sirtago with an expression of near awe. "He has been singled out by the gods. There could only be one reason for them to give a man so frightening a face. He must be a mighty warrior."

Poet smiled to himself. "Yes," he agreed. "A mighty warrior." Warrior, yes. but mighty... not yet. Sirtago could be a great many things, but his anger was like a fire and it often burned out of control.

"Tell me of the battles you fought in," Ramel demanded. So Poet did, and, as he was the Poet, he told the story the way it should have happened, rather than the way that it did. Poet had an appreciative audience and in his ears mishaps, bad decisions and poor planning became a tale of adventure, tempestuous circumstances and triumph. Poet told the tale minus the blood, the dirt and the dysentary.

The afternoon was wearing on. They had not stopped moving since the dawn and now the sun was getting low in the western sky. They crested a small hill and were almost to the bottom of the downslope when Sirtago stopped.

Poet moved his beast alongside Sirtago. "We could make the Ibarran border by nightfall if we..."

"Quiet!" Sirtago growled, holding up a clenched fist for emphasis. Poet closed his mouth and listened.

"Why have we stopped?" asked Ramel as he joined the others. Both Poet and Sirtago turned and 'shushed' him. Poet strained his ears. He could hear something. He could hear movement and he thought he could hear low voices whispering in a gutteral language.

"Tey'ei...?" Poet whispered.

Sirtago nodded. He motioned for Poet and Ramel to remain where they were and with a swiftness and a silence that belied his size, Sirtago slipped from his mount and climbed back up the hill they had just descended.

Ramel inched his camel closer to Poet's. "What is it?" he whispered.

Poet was still staring up the hill where Sirtago had gone. He could not see him, nor could he hear his progress, but he could still detect the faint sounds of movement — footfalls and low voices. "There may be a Tey'ei patrol nearby," Poet explained. "Sirtago has gone to scout their position. He will determine where they are headed and then decide the best route for us to take to avoid them."

"Avoid them?" Ramel blurted, rather loudly. "Why would we...?"

"Be quiet!" Poet hissed. "There are only three of us! We're no match for a Tey'ei patrol!"

Suddenly the air was split with a bloodcurdling cry. Ramel started and his face showed fear. Poet's heart sank when he heard the cry, for he knew what it was. Sirtago had gone into battle.

"Come on..." Poet said, slipping from his mount. He did not stop to see if Ramel followed but scrambled up the hill as fast as he could.

At the crest he looked back the way they had come and saw Sirtago swinging his blade in a frenzied arc. One Tey'ei soldier in the black armour of a patrol guard lay dead at his feet and five others were approaching.

Sirtago's blade caught the first of the Tey'ei to approach and opened up the man's chest. Sirtago gave another mighty swing but the third stepped back, away from the blade's deadly arc.

Poet knew that Sirtago could keep up that movement, what the Trigassan sword masters called 'the Whirling Death', for hours, far longer than was possible for most men. Poet also knew that in that time many more Tey'ei might arrive.

Drawing his twin long knives Poet ran down the other side of the hill to join the fray. Poet did not have near the strength that Sirtago posessed, but his blades were quick and deadly accurate. Poet knew ways to kill with a single thrust.

Poet sliced and stabbed at two of the Tey'ei. He dodged the ugly, serrated blade of a third before piercing the fellow's throat with a lightning stab.

Poet whirled around. There was no one in sight but six dead Tey'ei and Sirtago, his blood lust still causing his great shoulders to heave. "They must have been closer than we thought," Poet said.

"They were following us," Sirtago managed through clenched teeth. "Abominations! They are a scourge... a plague that needs wiping out."

Poet relaxed his stance and sheathed his daggers. "That's Ussan's philosophy, not yours, Sirtago, and I doubt that Ussan *really* believes it."

Sirtago shook his head. He was becoming calmer. "The Tey'ei should not be here in the Nats'n. They should go back to their own land and practice their wicked ways on their own people."

Poet sighed. "They won't leave these lands. Not as long as there is Ootin for them to steal."

"It is ours! They steal it from us."

"It's not ours, Sirtago. Trigassa has no Ootin."

"The Ibarra does."

Poet nodded. He could see the last of Sirtago's blood lust draining from him. "Ibarra has more Ootin than anyone, and they sell it to those who can pay the price. That is why it is such a rich kingdom. Rich in gold, flowing wine, sweatmeats — and women."

Sirtago nodded. "Aye... women."

Poet smiled. He knew Sirtago well. He knew his friend's interests and what would lure him on.

Poet opened his mouth to speak when the sound of clashing steel came to their ears. Poet looked around him. "Where is Ramel?"

Sirtago's placid features tightened into an angry glare. He dashed back up the hill, Poet at his heels.

On the other side of the hill were six more Tey'ei. They surrounded Ramel who was desparately sparring with the patrol leader. The man's ugly blade moved quickly and accurately, easily parrying Ramel's clumsy thrusts. The other Tey'ei watched in amusement.

Sirtago let out a thunderous roar and descended on the patrol. Poet whipped out his knives and joined the fight.

Poet dispatched a surprised patrolman and glanced at Ramel.

The leader had become distracted by Sirtago's charge and Poet saw Ramel push his blade forward. Ramel's thrust was accurate despite his inexperience. His blade penetrated the leader's side and sank deep, almost to the hilt.

"Well done, Ramel!" Poet shouted and moved to dispatch two more Tey'ei.

Sirtago continued his roaring and his Whirling Death. Poet risked a glance back at Ramel. The lad had not moved. His sword had slid from the leader's insides as he fell dead and Ramel stared at the blood-soaked blade.

The youth was transfixed. His eyes were wide as plates and Poet suddenly knew, in a flash of insight that Ramel had never killed anyone before. "Keep fighting, Ramel!" Poet shouted as he dodged a Tey'ei blade.

It was no good. Ramel was rooted to the spot in disbelief of what he had done.

Suddenly one of the Tey'ei grabbed Ramel, and held his blade to the young man's throat.

"NO!" Poet shouted. He ran to Ramel.

"That's far enough!" the Tey'ei growled in a heavily accented Nats'ni. "Drop your weapons or this whelp will die!"

Poet froze. The Tey'ei was a brutish looking man. His face sported a long scar and his greasy black hair hung to his shoulders. Poet saw in the patrolman's eyes that he spoke the truth. He would just as soon kill a boy as spit on the ground.

Poet felt a sudden great pain, as if he had been struck hard in the back. He threw back his head and shouted once, then looked down to see the point of a serrated blade sticking out from his belly and covered with his own blood.

Poet stared in horrid fascination as the point withdrew back into his belly. He looked up and on the crest of the hill stood a figure in flowing black robes. It was a woman with hair the colour of fire and skin the colour of milk. She stood motionless, staring intently at Poet as he dropped to his knees in the sand.

Poet surmised that this was death. Poet knew death would be frightening, and she was, but he had not expected her to be beautiful as well. Life was full of surprises, Poet reflected as he fell forward onto the desert floor and blackness claimed him.

2. SORCERESS

AN ODD green glow. Visions — blurry and confused — memories?

Lying on his back — the world moving around him, the sun bathing the air in a fiery glow. Sirtago, his head bloodied, his eyes unfocused. "We would not be here," Poet heard his own voice speaking. "...but for you. Why do you evade your responsibilities? You cannot run away from yourself."

"Shut up..." Sirtago mumbling back. "Have the decency to die in silence. Why do you pester me like a fly?"

...now cold. Darkness, cold and close. Stone walls. A long tunnel. Again the world moved around him. He could see the back of a black armoured Tey'ei soldier. He was carrying something that Poet's legs rested upon.

...a face. Death. Long, fiery hair... white skin and green eyes. Death moves around him... touches him with cold hands... washes him. Why does death take so long? Why can Poet not see the afterlife? "Where is *Sonne*?" Poet asks. "Why can I not see her garden?"

"Lie still," is Death's only response.

Now green. Not the green of leaves but a pale, sick green glow of something unnatural. Poet feels pain. His body is stiff and his midriff is bound in white cloth. His clothes are gone.

POET OPENED his eyes and saw his surroundings clearly for the first time. He was in a cold stone room with low arches. The stone was dark and grey and the blocks were uneven. He turned his head and saw a round glass vial filled with a liquid. Swimming in the liquid were several long worms whose bodies gave off a greenish glow. The glowing worms were the room's only source of light. Poet stared in fascination at the wriggling things as they swarmed and squirmed around each other.

"They live deep in the Ootin caves," a voice said. Poet turned his head and saw the woman with the fiery hair standing over him. "They never see the light of the sun so their bodies make light."

Poet shook his head. His neck was stiff and he could feel a dull, throbbing pain throughout his body. "You are not death." he managed to say.

The woman smiled an unpleasant smile. "I am Himrassa," she said. Her voice was strong, yet womanish, but it sent a chill down Poet's spine to hear the dark power beneath it. "Who is *Sonne*?"

Poet's brow furrowed. "Sonne is the goddess of letters. Scholars and Poets pay homage to her. After we die we spend eternity in Sonne's garden, writing and discussing..." A sudden wave of nausea forced him to stop.

Himrassa's lips curled into a self-satisfied smile. "A quaint superstition. How fascinating you Nats'n are."

"I'm not Nats'n. I am Trigassan."

"I have never heard of Trigassa," Himrassa said, bemused. "It doesn't matter. You are here now."

"I was stabbed," Poet said, the memory of the Tey'ei blade through his stomach coming back to him. "I died."

Himrassa shook her head. "Almost. I brought you back."

"You are a healer?"

In response the woman chuckled deep in her throat and again something in her voice made Poet shiver. "You are a man of letters, I take it?"

"I am Poet. Such is my vocation. Such is my name." Poet lifted his head and looked around the chamber. There were vials filled with unidentifiable substances. He saw an Ootin globe resting on a stone table. Beside it was another, broken into small pieces. Suddenly, he understood. "You are a sorceress," he said.

Himrassa nodded. "You understand the uses for the Ootin? Good."

"Where is Sirtago?" he asked. He remembered a vison — was it a dream or a memory? — Sirtago with a bloodied head.

Himrassa made a dismissive gesture. "Your companion is of no concern. I have told the guards not to hurt him."

"Ramel...?"

Her smile widened, and Poet found he did not like the look of that. "Your young friend is well and safe from harm. Try to stand."

Poet lifted himself up and slowly managed to swing his legs over the edge of the stone slab upon which he had been lying. His body protested, not so much from pain but from not being used for such a long while. He wondered how long he had lain here unmoving.

He put his feet down on the cold stone floor and stood, keeping one hand on the table for balance. The white dressing around his belly was his only covering. He shivered in the cold.

"Good. Your strength has returned." Himrasa said. She was tall, like all Tey'ei, and she radiated a sense of power. She looked Poet up and down, seemingly satisfied. "You will want clothing. I will fetch you some."

She turned to go and Poet saw his long daggers resting on a small bench. He was stiff from inactivity, but her back was to him and he may never get another chance. In a swift, but inelegant move, Poet scooped up a dagger and raised it to strike.

His arm would not move. He willed the dagger to thrust. He imagined it piercing the black robe and stabbing the sorceress, but his body refused to obey the command of his will.

Himrassa turned back towards him and gazed amusedly at the dagger quivering mere inches from her. She smiled and opened her robe. Underneath she wore a halter and a low slung skirt. Poet could see the delicate, alabaster skin of her throat, her breast, and below the gentle curve of her stomach, tantalizingly exposed. Still the dagger would not move.

"Do you think me a fool?" Himrassa asked. "Do you seriously think that I would bring back an enemy of the Tey'ei to life without protecting myself. You can no more kill me than you could kill yourself."

Poet allowed the dagger to drop to his side. The attempt had taken all of his strength. He slumped and leaned back against the table. "How have you done this?" he asked between breaths.

Himrassa laughed and there was something deep underneath the tone of her laughter that disturbed Poet to his very core. "Human minds —" she explained. "Especially male human minds — are very pliable. They are easily susceptible to my sorcery."

The dagger slipped from the loose grip that Poet could barely keep on it and it clattered to the stone floor. "You have bewitched me."

"Indeed, I have," Himrassa said. She stooped and picked up the dagger from the floor, casually tossing it back with its companion on the bench.

As she rose she moved closer to Poet. She gazed down at him and he saw a look in her eyes. A hunger — a lust. She moved her face closer to his. Poet could not move out of the way if he wanted to.

Then she turned away and picked up her robe, covering herself with it as she retreated. "Rest," she commanded. She moved to a small door and opened it just enough to allow herself to slip through. Beyond the door Poet caught a glimpse of an orange light that bathed Himrassa's pale features. For an instant he saw that look again, like the look of one who has gone for too long without food.

Then the door closed and Poet was left alone in the cold darkness.

He leaned against the stone table for a while. He felt very weak and dizzy. He watched the glowing worms swimming in the vial. It was the only thing in the room that he could see clearly.

Where was Sirtago? He must be imprisoned somewhere. If Sirtago were loose Poet had no doubt that he would hear him. Were he loose he would be causing as much havoc as he could. Himrassa said that she had told the guards not to hurt him. The

Tey'ei respected their sorcerers, but Poet knew that Sirtago was not easily kept under lock and key.

He had to find out where Sirtago was. He had to find Ramel as well. If he was alive someplace Poet had to find him and bring him home safely. He thought wistfully of flowing wine and plentiful sweetmeats in Ibarra. He thrust the thought away. For now his main goal was to remain alive and escape, if escape was possible.

Poet explored the large stone room, carefully noting all the vials and trying to identify their contents. There were many books as well, old scrolls, some covered with many years' worth of desert sand.

In the corner he found a bunk. It was a wooden shelf, but it was stuffed with straw and hastily covered with a blanket. It was much more comfortable than the stone table on which he'd awoken so he lay down. He still felt weak from his wounds and he fell into a troubled sleep.

He was awakened by the sound of the room's outer door. He opened his eyes and saw an old Tey'ei man stepping into the room, bearing a tray. The old man shuffled across to Himrassa's inner chamber and knocked. Poet could hear Himrassa's voice say something in Tey'ei and the old man opened the inner door and shuffled in.

Poet was about to close his eyes and return to sleep when he saw that the chamber's outer door was left opened. Poet was suddenly fully awake. He stared at the open door. If he could get up fast enough, scramble through the room without making a sound, he could slip unnoticed through the outer door, find Sirtago, find Ramel and make their escape.

He had just resolved to leap up and go when the old man returned from the inner chamber and shuffled across the floor. Through barely open eyes Poet watched as the old Tey'ei moved back through the outer door, closing off Poet's one chance of escape.

LATER ON Himrassa emerged from the inner chamber. She

deemed different to Poet — rested — fed. She wore a self-satisfied smile that made Poet nervous.

"You slept?" she asked.

Poet nodded.

"Good. I have a task for you to perform." She opened a wooden box and drew from it several old scrolls. "Can you read this?" Himrassa handed him one of the scrolls.

Poet could not tell how ancient the writings were. The parchment was torn and dirty with time and the writing itself was nearly faded. It was a variant of Nats'n Aug writing. Poet surmised that it was ancient in form. He began to read aloud. "*Through the circle of Kalesh and round the stars of the holy...*" Poet looked up. Himrassa was writing out the words that he spoke on a new parchment in blocky Tey'ei script.

"Go on," she said, not looking up from her own paper. Poet continued.

The manuscript was the account of a scholar who lived in the Nats'n many centuries ago. Much of it was confusing to Poet, but it spoke of the discovery of a fissure in the earth into which a powerful sorcerer, referred to only as 'The Mad One', had imprisoned a powerful and frightening being called *K'tu*. The scholar was meticulous in the details of the locks and the incantations used to seal up the fissure.

After the fissure was sealed it was buried in the sand. The rest of the manuscript contained long and prodigious thanks to the gods for their safe journey as well as a comprehensive account of the number of their company and the contents of each of their packs.

Poet read through the document aloud several times while Himrassa translated. Finally she sat, staring at her parchment, a sour expression on her face. "Is there nothing in the scrolls about how K'tu was imprisoned in the first place?"

Poet shrugged. "The scrolls are incomplete. We have the end of the account but not the beginning."

Himrassa thinned her lips and regarded Poet with a piercing expression. Poet tried to meet her gaze steady on, but her eyes had a burning fire in them that Poet found discomforting. His eyes dropped to the text. He read the word *Ch'achant'gha*. In modern day Nats'ni it meant *to imprison*. But it did have an ancient meaning. "There might be a clue," Poet said aloud. He looked up at Himrassa. Her expression softened.

"Where?" she asked.

Poet tapped the scroll. "This word — *Ch'achant'gha*. It's derived from an old Nats'n word — *Ch'achant'iseya*. It means something like *binding exchange*. It's an old practice whereby captured leaders give up something as a token of their surrender. The victorious leader, in place of slaying a respected opponent, would take something from him. In ancient times it might have been a body part — a finger or an ear — then it became items like swords. When the conquered foe was released — when the *Ch'achant'iseya* pact was dissolved — the item was returned along with a small item from the conquering leader. Nowadays it would be a token like a ring or a jewel. In ancient times the dissolution of the pact would require blood."

Himrassa stared at him, her eyes wide and intense. "Yes," she said. She flipped through the parchment she'd marked with her own Tey'ei script. "Back here where the scholar lists the admonitions. '*Neither shall there be duelling or killing*,'" she read. "'*The opening of the skin shall be forbidden. Neither shall we suffer women in whom the time is strong*'. That must be a reference to a woman's blood cycle. There was to be no spilling of blood near the imprisoned K'tu."

Poet sat back. "The sorcerer must have taken something from K'tu while uttering an imprisonment charm. The only way to release K'tu would be with the return of that item and a sacrifice of blood."

Himrassa smiled a wide and wicked smile. She stood up, moved across the room and reached into another wooden box. From within she pulled out an object wrapped in an old rag. She set it down on the table and pulled away the rag revealing a glass jar that glowed green. Inside the jar was a murky liquid. Poet stared, fascinated and yet horrified at the thick substance that swirled and danced within the jar.

The liquid contained small whitish grey flecks and Poet moved closer to the jar to get a better look at them. As he did so a round white object rolled around within thc glass. It moved unerringly close to Poet's face and rolled around to reveal an eye which stared horridly up at Poet.

Startled, Poet backed away, knocking over his stool as he did so and landing on his rump on the cold stone floor. Himrassa laughed at him, a high, piercing laugh that sent shivers up and down Poet's spine.

"A blood sacrifice," Himrassa crowed in awful triumph. "I should have known. I will give K'tu back her eye and free her. She will work my will — she will be a servant of the Tey'ei!"

Poet stared in sudden fright at this mad woman standing before him. Her face had taken on that look again — that hungry lustful look. She laughed again, hardly noticing Poet sprawled on the floor.

"Ramel," she said and strode towards the door to her inner chamber.

Poet started up. *Ramel*. Was he...?

Himrassa opened the door and Poet saw the familiar wash of orange light. This time, however, Himrassa did not close the door. Poet scrambled over and peered in through the narrow crack.

The inner chamber was smaller and narrower. The main feature was a bed on which a small naked figure was chained. It was Ramel.

Himrassa drank from a small cup. The liquid glowed with a faint orange light. Poet recognized it as *ootinage*, a deadly liquid made from the pulverised ootin. It was rumoured that sorcerers had developed a method to drink it safely.

The sorceress finished the ootinage and then dropped her outer robe and pulled a small needle from a vial. Carefully she held up the needle and moved it towards Ramel's exposed loin snake. She touched the needle to it, barely pricking the skin. Suddenly Ramel's member stood to attention. Himrassa replaced the needle, dropped her skirt and mounted the young man.

Poet watched in horrid fascination, ever mindful of the impropriety of his witness, but unable to tear his eyes away from the sight of the sorceress on top of Ramel, taking from him... for indeed, that was what she was doing... drawing from Ramel his youth, his vigour, his very life.

He saw Ramel gasp, his eyes flash open wide. Poet recognized the sounds of the young man ejecting his seed into the sorceress. Still, she did not stop writhing on top of him. The tincture with which she elicited the response in Ramel's member obviously would not let it subside with a mere spilling of seed. Himrassa drew from deeper and deeper within Ramel, drawing from him his vital life energies.

Finally satiated, Himrassa climbed off the young man and moved slowly and carefully to the back of her chamber. She opened a low door. From Poet's vantage point he could see that the door led into a low chamber which was illuminated by an orange glow.

Poet immediately recognized the Ootin light and saw what he supposed was the top curve of an Ootin globe. Himrassa wrapped herself around the globe, as if trying to draw warmth from it. Poet knew better, though, and knew now her reasons for siphoning so much life energy from Ramel. The ootinage that she had drunk was allowing her to transfer Ramel's life essence from her body to the ootin globe.

Poet had heard of such practices but had never seen it before. He stared in horrid fascination.

Why was she doing this? Was she going to drain Ramel of all his energies? If so, then what?

Poet looked at Ramel lying deflated on the bed. He was young and strong, but could not last forever. Soon he would be used up, and then...

Poet had to stifle a gasp. He had just convinced Himrassa that she would need a blood sacrifice to free K'tu. Would she sacrifice Ramel?

The idea startled Poet. Himrassa was mad—Poet felt that

deeply—he could hear it in her laughter, but was she mad enough to release a such demon?

Before he could decide Poet heard a noise from behind him. Himrassa's outer door was being opened from without.

Poet stole away from the inner door. He scrambled back to the wooden bunk in the corner of the room. Before he reached the bunk he caught sight of his daggers where Himrassa had casually laid them yesterday. So confident was she in her spell that she did not feel the need to put them away.

An idea formed inside Poet's head. He lay himself upon the bed and feigned sleep.

The moment he lay still the outer door opened. The old Tey'ei man entered as he had done yesterday, bearing a tray. As before the old man left the outer door open. He shuffled to the inner door and knocked. Poet heard Himrassa's voice speak in Tey'ei and the old man shuffled into the inner chamber.

Poet was up in a flash. He scooped his daggers from the bench and made a dash for the door.

Himrassa's chamber was at the end of a long and narrow stone corridor. Poet raced along the length of it. The floor was smooth and sloped downward.

There were doors along the length of the corridor. Some were open and Poet caught glimpses of Tey'ei men within. He did not slow or stop. He had to get out.

He spied a staircase that led down. He followed it. As he came to the bottom he caught the smell of food. Tey'ei cooking smells made his nose wrinkle, but his stomach rumbled in response anyway.

The stairway let out into a small kitchen. Old Tey'ei woman crowded around several cooking fires preparing a meal. Through the open door of the kitchen Poet could see a large eating area filled with Tey'ei soldiers. They were sitting down to a meal.

Poet scanned the kitchen and spied a smaller door on the opposite wall. Poet made for it but not before narrowly avoiding a collision with a small Tey'ei woman. The Tey'ei woman screamed at the sight of him and the kitchen's attention was suddenly on the him.

Poet ignored it and dashed through the inner door. He nearly fell down the stone steps on the other side. They curved as they descended and the air grew stale and dank.

Finally Poet reached the bottom. He was in a low, dark round chamber. There were cells along the wall. Poet had stumbled onto the dungeon.

He could hear voices moaning. In the cells he saw prisoners, some old and dessicated, some younger, eyeing Poet with a fierce intensity. Then Poet spied Sirtago.

He was in the far cell, sitting with his back against the wall, his head was down almost to his knees.

Poet rushed to the bars. "Sirtago!" he called. "Sirtago, it's me! It's Poet!"

Sirtago raised his head slowly. His head was bloodied. Sirtago's eye had a watery look and he seemed to have trouble seeing Poet. "Why am I taunted by the spirits of the dead?" Sirtago asked. His speech was slow and thick.

"Sirtago, it's me!" Poet said again in frustration. "I'm not dead!"

Sirtago shook his head and looked away. "First my father, now you. Will all those that are dead come and taunt me before the end?"

"Sirtago, I'm not dead!"

Sirtago shook his head wearily. "Poet, my dearest friend. Why could you not keep that loin snake of yours to yourself. We wouldn't be in this situation if you had..."

Sirtago's words provoked a sudden anger in Poet. "You're blaming me for this?" he asked, his voice raised. "You are the one who brought us here in the first place! If you had not evaded your responsibilities and gone off on this foolish quest of Cho Kassen's, we would still be in Trigassa!"

Poet's raised voice seemed to pain Sirtago. He held his head and began rocking back and forth. "My father is dead... I see his stern countenance before me even now. He mocks me, Poet... Oh, he mocks me..."

Poet calmed himself and rubbed his temples. "We don't even know for certain that your father is dead. He may still live."

"I see him, Poet..."

"You see your own fears, Sirtago. If the Emporer Joasim is dead, then you are Trigassa's first Emporer in Exile. We must go back — or at least get out of these cursed desert lands. In order to do that we must escape the Tey'ei. Listen to me, Sirtago!"

Sirtago looked at Poet. His eyes seemed to clear for a moment. It was as if he was seeing him for the first time. "Poet?" he said, hesitantly. "You *are* alive!"

Poet could not contain his laughter. "Yes, Sirtago. I am alive. And so are you and so is Ramel, but he won't be for long if we don't get out of here."

The cell had a large iron lock holding it closed. Poet examined the lock. He took his dagger and tried to insert it into the lock's keyhole. He could feel the mechanism within, but could not get the dagger deep enough within. "I need something else."

"You need the key." Sirtago said.

"I know that," Poet said, not taking his attention from his task of attempting to pick the lock. "I need something smaller... thinner."

From the corridor beyond Poet heard voices barking orders in Tey'ei. They would not have much time. Poet abandoned the lock and handed the dagger to Sirtago. Sirtago stared dumbly at the weapon for a moment before taking it and tucking it into his boot.

From behind him came a burst of Tey'ei. Poet recognized several curses. "Don't move!" a voice commanded.

Poet looked around slowly. Standing in front of a group of Tey'ei soldiers was the dark haired, evil looking Tey'ei they had fought in the desert. The one who had captured Ramel and forced their surrender. He was holding a long Tey'ei blade towards Poet.

"Stand up!" The Tey'ei commanded. Poet rose slowly, his hands in the air. His other dagger was on the floor beside his boot. The Tey'ei reached down and picked it up. As he did so he gave Poet an evil, hate-filled stare which made Poet shiver in spite of himself.

"Thank you, Captain," Himrassa's voice came from behind Poet. Poet saw a flash of disappointment on the captain's cruel face before he turned away to face the sorceress. Himrassa fixed Poet with a glare that was half wrathful and half amused. "You led us on a merry chase," she said. She held out her hand for Poet's dagger. The Captain handed it over.

"My lady," the captain said in a gravelly voice. "These prisoners are more trouble than they are worth. Let me kill them. They'll make good target practice for the men."

"No, Captain," Himrasa said smoothly, never taking her eyes off Poet. "I have other plans for both of them." She stepped closer to Poet. "I want you to see the liberation of K'tu. And I want to thank you for helping me to choose a blood sacrifice." Himrassa turned her gaze to Sirtago who was still swaying unsteadily in his cell.

"No," Poet protested. "You can't..."

"I do not want to give up Ramel," she interrupted his protest. "He is young and strong and will fulfill my needs for a year or more. A resource like that cannot be thrown away so casually." Now she returned her gaze to Poet and he felt himself transfixed under it. "You I like. You are different from these other rough desert people. Your mind and soul interest me. I will keep you as a souvenir of my time here. You will accompany me back to the Tey'ei Vaus along with K'tu. You will stay by my side as I wield K'tu's power and become empress of all the Tey'ei.

"But this one..." she indicated Sirtago. "I have no use for this one, except to help me release K'tu."

Poet looked into Himrassa's eyes and saw in them a madness that Poet dared not contemplate, lest he fall into it with her. He averted his eyes. He looked at Sirtago, still standing, albiet unsteadily, in his cell.

3. KTU

THE TEY'EI stronghold was built over what was thought at first to be an ootin cave. The entrance to the cave was in the center of the stronghold. The Tey'ei had built a high chamber around it. Directly above the aperture was a round opening that let in sunlight.

Now Himrassa led a party to the entrance of the cave. Tey'ei guards walked Sirtago unsteadily between them, the cruel captain leading, his evil serrated blade drawn.

Himrassa had Ramel by her side. He looked drawn and pale and he shrank and hid his eyes from the direct sunlight. Himrassa herself looked pale and seemed to shrink from the light, but in her eyes glowed a fierce intensity that Poet could not look upon. She cradled the eye of K'tu in her arms. The glass jar was once again wrapped in a cloth, but Poet could sense the malevolent presence of the organ.

Poet stood by Himrassa's side and cursed himself in every tongue that he knew. He had been a complete fool. He had thought that Himrassa had meant to sacrifice Ramel and had tried to enlist Sirtago's aid to save him. In doing so he had doomed Sirtago to death. He had doomed Sirtago's soul to eternal agony in Hell.

The party entered the cave. The way had been cleared over many years. A smooth path led in and downwards. As he entered the cave Poet felt the air grow suddenly cold against his skin and he shivered involuntarily.

Down, down the sloping path they went. Torches lit the way and created an acrid, black smoke that choked Poet as he walked, defeated beside the Sorceress.

"I'm cold," he heard Ramel say in a quiet, wavering voice. Himrassa put her arm around him, held the boy's head to her breast. Poet wondered at the seemingly tender gesture as Himrassa whispered into Ramel's ear. Poet shivered again as he remembered the sight of the sorceress drawing the life essence from the young man.

The tunnel narrowed and soon they came to a place where it had been deliberately blocked. A stone wall, a giant slab of rock, had been forced into the tunnel, blocking the way. The stone was covered in writing. Ancient Nats'ni words had been carved deeply into the surface of the stone. Much of it Poet recognized from the manuscript.

The party stopped. Himrassa gestured for the cruel Teyei captain to bring Sirtago forward. The officer pushed him towards the stone and forced Sirtago to his knees. It took some doing. The captain was shorter than Sirtago, and Poet's heart sank when he saw his friend forced down.

Himrassa took little notice. She put down the jar containing the eye of K'tu and pulled out the notes she had made back in her chamber. She began to speak, the ancient Nats'n words sounding strange coming from her Tey'ei tongue, yet she pronounced all carefully and with much precision.

She grew energised as she continued with the chant. Poet saw her lips curl into an evil smile in anticipation of the moment.

Poet began to feel a vibration, a thrumming that rose and fell like the rhythm of a man asleep and breathing deeply. As the vibration continued it seemed to get stronger. Poet could feel it rattling the bones in his chest. He could feel it dancing up over his skull.

The other Tey'ei felt it as well. Poet saw them beginning to shift and fidget in growing alarm.

Poet saw the ancient writing begin to glow on the stone slab. At first he thought it was an illusion created by flickering torchlight, but it was real. The writing itself began to burn within the rock, like forge fire. It flickered and moved redly, undulating over the stone.

The vibration had become a rumbling. Himrassa had to raise her voice in response to it, the ancient chant sounding louder and echoing inside the tunnel. She stooped and picked up the jar, unwrapping it from its cloth. Poet saw the murky liquid within roiling now, as if in agitation.

Himrassa placed the jar at the foot of the stone and backed away, all the time chanting the words that would unbind the creature that lay behind the rock.

Gradually the rumbling became a roar. Poet heard it and shivered involuntarily. It was like the roar of a giant beast or a jungle cat. It was like the scream of old women and like the wail of infants. It was like a scream of fear and a roar of triumph, yet unlike any sound that Poet had ever heard in his life.

Suddenly the stone slab disappeared. It did not crumble or break. One instant it was there, solid, blocking the tunnel and the next instant it was gone.

The screaming and rumbling grew louder. The Tey'ei soldiers were openly agitated now. Naked fear showed on their faces, even the cruel captain's.

Poet glanced at Ramel who was cowering with fright behind Himrassa. Poet felt fear from his shoes to his head. Only Sirtago seemed unmoved by the roaring of the demon. He weaved unsteadily, his hands manacled in front of him, but Poet thought he could see his hands flexing.

Poet's attention was suddenly drawn to movement. Something black and wet slithered from out of the darkness of the tunnel. It wrapped itself around the glass jar and drew it back out of the light.

Poet's eyes were round with disbelief. He had seen demons before, but never had he seen anything so monstrous.

A thunderous roar shook the cave, louder and more fierce than any that came before. Suddenly K'tu herself was there.

She was black. Blacker than any starless night Poet had ever seen. Her many arms weaved and danced in front of her and when she roared the tunnel shook. Flecks of the same white goo that had been in Himrassa's jar spattered the tunnel floor in front of her. She was an awesome sight to behold. She was not snake nor insect nor fish nor fowl. She was none of these things and all of these things all at the same time.

Now the Tey'ei were gripped with abject fear. Even the cruel captain stood transfixed by this horror. His serrated blade was out and ready to dispatch Sirtago on a command from the sorceress, but it was forgotten. He stared at K'tu like a man stares at his own doom.

Himrassa's grin had widened. She was pulsing with excitement. She could barely finish the incantation. Her voice had risen to a fever pitch. Poet heard her shouting in ancient Nats'ni: "Take of me this gift, given freely, great K'tu!"

That was the phrase the Tey'ei captain had been instructed to listen for, but he was so transfixed on the monstrosity in front of him he had forgotten his duty to dispatch Sirtago at the appointed time.

Now a great wind began to blow inside the tunnel. The wind moved down the tunnel, towards the demon. Himrassa's hair began to fly wildly about her head. "TAKE OF ME THIS GIFT..." she shouted at the Tey'ei captain, trying to jar him out of his apoplexy. "...GIVEN FREELY, GREAT K'TU!"

The Tey'ei captain dragged his eyes from the demon and met Himrassa's glare. He raised his blade to strike Sirtago, but it was too late.

Sirtago had used that moment of hesitation. Only Poet saw him reach into his boot and pull out the dagger that Poet had given him. With a motion almost too quick to follow Sirtago whipped the blade up and drove it into Himrassa's side.

The sorceress let out a scream. Immediately her blood began to stream out of her. It followed the course of the wind. A tiny rivulet of crimson flowed from her side towards the great demon.

The motion startled the captain. He swung his sword.

"Sirtago, LOOK OUT!" Poet screamed. He did not know if Sirtago even heard him over the rushing of wind and the roaring of the demon, but he turned as the captain's blade arced downward. He held out his wrists. The blade caught the short length of chain that connected the manacles around Sirtago's wrists. The blade broke the chain and Sirtago was up on his feet, rushing the startled captain.

All hell, and K'tu, broke loose. The demon advanced. A black arm grabbed Himrassa and with a clean jerk pulled the sorceress towards her. Poet saw a maw open up and swallow Himrassa whole.

The Tey'ei soldiers lost their nerve then. They bolted back up the tunnel. Sirtago knocked the captain down with his shoulder. The captain took one look at the advancing demon and let out a womanish scream that echoed around the tunnel. His blade slipped, forgotten from his fingers as he tried to scramble away.

Sirtago grabbed the fallen blade and swung it at the advancing demon just as her many-jointed black arms were reaching for him. The blade snapped cleanly through two of them. Thick black blood began to flow and the white, stringy substance was flung everywhere. K'tu screamed and the sound shook the tunnel so violently Poet thought that it would collapse upon them all.

Poet shook himself to action. He grabbed Ramel who was cowering by the tunnel wall. He dragged the lad to his feet. "Sirtago, RUN!" he managed to shout back over his shoulder, then took off back up the tunnel.

Poet looked back once to see Sirtago running behind them, then he turned and made for the surface as fast as he could. They came to the cave mouth only to discover the outside world plunged into darkness. The sun had set as they had been below the earth.

Ramel collapsed onto the sand. Poet was about to join him when a thunderous roar sounded from the tunnel mouth. Poet saw Sirtago emerging backwards, the Tey'ei blade swinging before him in the Whirling Death, and the demon K'tu following behind.

A shriek erupted from Poet's lips at the sight of the monstrosity above ground. Its many black arms whirled and feinted. Sirtago's blade connected with arms that got too close. He hacked pieces of the demon left and right but still it continued to advance on him.

Poet looked desperately for any avenue of escape for his friends. He saw the Tey'ei compound. The door out of which they had emerged stood wide open. The Tey'ei soldiers were undoubtedly inside. Perhaps they were arming to combat the demon. More likely they were cowering in fear.

"Sirtago!" Poet shouted. "Make for the compound!" And he grabbed Ramel and ran for the open door.

Inside there was no sign of the Tey'ei soldiers. Poet stopped and watched as Sirtago broke from combat with the demon and ran for the open doorway. As soon as he was inside Poet slammed shut the heavy wooden door. Sirtago picked up the bar and set it in its place, locking it against entry.

But the demon would not be held back for long. The stronghold shook with another thunderous roar from just outside the door. The heavy barricade trembled and immediately began to buckle.

"It would take an army to stop this demon!" Sirtago shouted. "Where are those Tey'ei bastards?"

Poet shook his head. "You cannot defeat it with a force of arms. Only sorcery can..."

"We don't have any sorcrery. That sorceress bitch is dead!"

Another thunderous roar and the door shook and buckled again. It would not hold the demon outside for long.

Suddenly Poet had an idea. "The sorceress is dead, but some of her power may still be alive." He turned and ran back inside the complex.

"Where are you going?" Sirtago shouted at him, but Poet ignored him. He had to find Himrassa's room.

He had only seen the inside of the complex once. His headlong flight to rescue Sirtago had not afforded him much opportunity to study the layout of the stronghold.

Poet ran, turning corners that looked familiar. He finally found himself in front of Himrassa's chambers. He ran through the outer room, into the recessed chamber and finally down to the secret room and the ootin globe.

The room was small and cold. The ootin globe gave off a steady orange pulse of light but it gave off no heat. It seemed rather to draw the heat from the room into itself. Poet laid a hand upon it. It was cold and it made the hairs on Poet's body stand on end.

He ignored that. He pushed at the ootin globe. It was on a small stand, like a pedestal. Poet tried to roll it off the pedestal, but it was heavy and resisted. He needed Sirtago's strength, but Sirtago was holding off a demon.

Desperate now, Poet braced himself for one final heave. Suddenly the globe lurched off the pedestal, as if of its own volition. It rolled off the edge and fell to the floor. Instead of the loud thump, and perhaps the crash that Poet had expected, there was nothing. The globe looked like it was sitting on the stone floor of the inner chamber, but when he looked closer he saw that it hovered a mere breath away from the surface.

Poet did not waste time wondering at the ootin globe's magic, for he had reasoned that much of Himrassa's sorcery, as well as the life essence of Ramel and perhaps countless numbers of Himrassa's other victims, now resided within the globe.

Poet began to roll the globe and it moved easily, even up the stone steps. Out the door, through the bed chamber, through the larger chamber and into the hallway. The globe itself seemed to sense its destination and seemed eager to greet it.

Soon Poet was running to keep up with the rolling globe. He guided it around a corner and was startled to see a group of Tey'ei soldiers. The had overcome their fear and had armed themselves for combat with the demon that was now invading their compound.

There was barely time for one of the Tey'ei to shout in alarm, however, before they were all bowled over by the rolling ootin globe. It knocked the Tey'ei out of its way as if they were not there and just kept on rolling. Poet scrambled to stay in its wake.

Poet guided it around corners and up to the entrance room. Ahead he could hear the sudden sound of a breaking door and another mighty roar, the challenge call of K'tu. He heard Sirtago answer the roar with one of his own and knew that he had to hurry.

He rolled the globe around the final corner and saw Sirtago

with the Tey'ei blade whirling death around him. K'tu pressed an attack from all sides and Sirtago lopped off black limbs left and right.

K'tu let out an angry roar and advanced on Sirtago. One arm snaked past Sirtago's whirling blade. It was reaching for Ramel who was huddled in a corner.

Ramel saw the black appendage undulating towards him and let out a screech. Poet gave the ootin globe a final shove, rolling it towards the fearful demon.

"SIRTAGO, LOOK OUT!" Poet shouted. Sirtago swung his blade once before the globe caught him behind his knees and he tumbled over backwards. Sirtago landed on the stone floor with a thump. The ootin globe continued to roll towards K'tu.

Sirtago was back on his feet and roaring with anger. He held his blade high. K'tu grasped the ootin globe. The demon's attention seemed to be rivited by the globe which was now glowing a bright orange.

"Sirtago, RUN!" Poet shouted. "Get out of there!" Poet grabbed Ramel and withdrew back into the complex.

Sirtago swung down with his sword. The Tey'ei blade struck the ootin globe held in K'tu's arms and shattered.

For a moment they were frozen there like that. Poet saw it all happen slowly. Sirtago holding the handle of the shattered blade, his anger slowly being replaced by an expression of dread. K'tu's attention was still focused on the ootin globe. The demon's great maw opened as if it meant to eat the thing.

The globe began to break. Poet could hear the sound of cracking and popping. A great fissure opened up where Sirtago's blade had shattered.

Suddenly the globe exploded into a dazzling display of the brightest light Poet had ever seen. He closed his eyes reflexively against the glare.

His ears were assaulted with a sound like the sudden rush of a wild storm. A loud crack like thunder sounded and Poet found himself pushed back by a force that knocked the wind from his lungs.

Poet held Ramel close as the world seemed to tear itself apart around him. For a brief moment Poet could not tell which direction was up or which was down. He tried to close his eyes against the bright glare, but he could still see it through his closed eyelids, flashing and beaming like the worst lightning storm he had ever seen.

Then fell what felt like hail all around them. The noise had dissipated and the light had gone. Now all was black and Poet could only hear the awful ringing in his own ears.

He stayed like that for the longest time, hunched over, covering Ramel, before daring to open his eyes. He was covered with dust and dirt. The floor around him was littered with tiny broken stones. He looked up and saw the stars shining coldly in the night sky.

The entire front entrance to the Tey'ei's stronghold was gone. It was obliterated, smashed into tiny pebbles.

There was no sign of K'tu, or the ootin globe, or of Sirtago.

Poet stood. Small pieces of stone fell from his clothes as he did so. Ramel stood as well. They walked out into the now open space. All that remained was the floor except for where K'tu had been. A great blackened hole was the only thing left of the demon.

Poet gazed around himself, stunned. There were small pieces of the compound scattered widely over the desert. Of the ootin globe or K'tu there was nothing. There was only the bright, clean fingers of dawn emerging in the eastern sky.

Then Poet spied Sirtago's body.

He lay on the desert floor where the explosion had hurled him. His legs were bent at an unnatural angle. One arm was flung before him. His other was pinned under his body.

Poet felt the shock hit him like being suddenly doused with cold water. His friend... his almost brother... was dead.

Slowly he began to walk towards Sirtago's corpse. Poet felt a numbness begin to creep over him. He drew closer and Sirtago lay still and unmoving.

As he stood over the body of his friend Poet felt a single tear trickle down his cheek.

Then Sirtago took in a huge, shuddering breath. He pushed himself up, rolled himself over, his scarred visage facing up to the sky. His one eye opened. "*Sonne's Tits*!" he breathed.

"SIRTAGO!" Poet shouted in shock and alarm.

Sirtago glanced up at Poet who he'd only just noticed was standing there. "What?"

Poet frowned at Sirtago's prone form. "Don't blaspheme," he admonished.

Sirtago stared at Poet for a moment in disbelief. Then he began to laugh. Sirtago laughed loud and long.

It was the sweetest sound that Poet had ever heard.

IT WASN'T long before the Tey'ei soldiers began to emerge from the compound, blinking in shock at the incredible devastation in the rosy dawn light. That was Poet and Sirtago's cue to leave quietly.

The camels that had been stabled nearby had been frightened by the explosion and had scattered into the desert. Poet and Sirtago gathered them up. Many were saddled and some had travel packs. Poet gathered as many of these as he could carry and they made off again towards the Eidos Ibarra.

They travelled for many days but did not encounter any more Tey'ei. They crossed the borders of the desert and soon were in the lush lands of Ramel's country.

They arrived at the Cho Kassen palace and were welcomed ecstatically. The Cho Kassen family had feared greatly for Ramel's life and were overjoyed to have their youngest son back. They promised Poet and Sirtago the riches of the kingdom.

"Today is a day of double happiness!" the elder Cho Kassen proclaimed. He was dressed in finest silks and gold brocade. Poet felt uncomfortably shabby next to him. He and Sirtago were covered with sand, grit, dried blood and bad odour.

The elder Cho Kassen led them into his chamber. Standing in the center of a small group was what Poet at first took to be a tall, dark haired Tey'ei. Both he and Sirtago stopped and stiffened at the sight of him.

The elder Cho Kassen approached him and bowed. "Your eminence," he said. "These..." he turned and indicated Poet and Sirtago. "...are two of our Kajaghn fighters, newly returned from the Nats'n front."

The tall dark Tey'ei narrowed his eyes at Poet and Sirtago, but then smiled a wide and disingenuous smile. "A pleasure to meet two such fine men," he said in a strange accent.

"This is the emperor of the N'Chirem," Cho Kassen explained. "The great enemy of the Tey'ei."

Poet regarded the emperor. He had never seen a N'Chirem. He had only been told stories of their powerful sorcery and their depraved and despotic ways.

"Have you killed many Tey'ei?" The emporer asked.

"We destroyed a Tey'ei stronghold," Sirtago answered slowly, uncertainly. "I killed a Tey'ei sorceress."

The N'Chirem emperor's smile widened. "Excellent. That is excellent. It is so heart warming to see such dedication from our Nats'n friends."

"We're not Nats'n," Poet said. "We're Trigassan."

The emporer frowned. "Trigassan?" He turned back to the crowd behind him. "Wasn't one of your ambassadors from Trigassa?"

"He was indeed," said one of the crowd, coming forth, his arms outstretched. He wore Trigassan robes and was covered in royal sashes and tokens. Poet did not recognize him until he approached.

"Firrule?" Sirtago said. He looked closer to see that it was indeed his cousin.

"It is so good to see you, Sirtago!"

Sirtago looked suddenly uncomfortable. "How is Trigassa?" he asked, warily. "How does my mother and my sister?"

"The empress is well. Your sister's belly swells with her child and your father is overjoyed."

"My father? He is alive?"

Firrule frowned. "Of course he is alive. He is well and

healthy."

Sirtago scowled in puzzlement. "When I left he was near death."

"No," Firrule said, shaking his head and smiling. "I was there with the physician. He passed a stone as big as my thumb right through his loin snake." Firrule shuddered and laughed. "If I had not seen it I would not have believed it. But once the stone passed he was fine. He has been well ever since."

Sirtago and Poet exchanged glances. Sirtago's flight into the desert, their joining the kajaghn fighters... it had all been for nothing.

The group began to move. Before he left the N'Chirem emperor smiled once more at Poet and Sirtago. "Keep up the fight." he said. "We can't allow Tey'ei aggression to spread any further," and then he was gone.

Firrule followed. "I must attend the meeting," he explained. "Dine with me tonight. You can return to Trigassa with me."

Sirtago nodded as Firrule disappeared. They were alone.

The back of the room opened up into a small garden with a fountain. Poet shuffled over to it and sat, letting the cooling spray from the fountain mist him with dew.

"I'm going to find a bath," Sirtago said. "Cho Kassen said I could have access to his harem. And wine. I want wine."

When Sirtago had left, Poet closed his eyes. Firrule had said that Jeswana was with child. It had broken his heart when she had married. Now that pain came back to him as stongly and as fiercly as it had before.

He thought about the Tey'ei and the N'Chirem and their war that he had been fighting for the last month. He thought about Ussan Cho Kassen and his Kajaghn who thought they were fighting for independence. They were merely pieces in a game being played between the N'Chirem and the Tey'ei.

Poet sighed. He knew he would return to Trigassa with Sirtago. He knew his heart would break again when he saw Jeswana carrying another man's child, but he would go with Sirtago. After all, he was merely a piece in Sirtago's game. ✱

The Deathmaster's Folly

G. W. Thomas

It is odd writing an intro to your own story but it does give you an advantage as well. I know why I wrote it and its evolution intimately. This story came out of the process of putting together the Magistria *shared world anthology (www.ricassopress.com Buy a copy!). My story in that book featured "death mages", sorcerers who used necromancy as their element. My original idea had the hero going all the way to their wicked city and being horrified by the sickening science of the undead. What I went with in the end was a truncated version that didn't please the critics or myself. So I came back to the idea but challenged myself to make the sorcerers be the heroes! And so the adventures of*

Fauston and Ramid grew from a simple journey to a doom-filled fate. The three sections here form the first half of their story. The rest is part of my upcoming book, The Gods Have Left Us.

Part One: The Road To Shan

"The road to Hell is made of little steps." – Torinde

THE HIGH-PITCHED yodel of a thanator keened through Fauston's open window. He took no notice of the song, which praised the Nineteen Missing Gods of Death and their one hundred and twenty-seven visages. Fauston heard the same song every hour on the hour. Only if the singer were particularly good or wretched would he have noticed. This song-spinner was competent, so therefore unremarkable.

The necromancer ignored the window and the bustling streets outside it. His attention was rapt on a vellum scroll bearing the script of the North. He knew the language well enough for a rough translation but now pondered certain words unknown to him. 'Jabiscul'—was it 'farmer' or 'serf'? And 'buramiscon' – was it 'army' or "

'soldiers'? Either way the letter came with a small chest of five hundred plats from Ghand.

And this was just a sweetener, mused the mage. Baron Breka would pay handsomely for his services. But that meant leaving the bazaars and cotillions of Riin. Could he bear to miss Sir Gahout's Dance of the Dead, when forty mages would resurrect all those buried in the city's cemetery to dance the entire night? To miss that was an unthinkable faux pas. Still, there was the chest of coins…

He looked at the sum at the bottom of the scroll again. Fifty thousand plats. Even at Riin's exchange rates that was still over thirty thousand skels. Enough to pay all of Fauston's debts plus the special project…

Fauston tossed the scroll onto the floor. His thoughts had turned to Rayahl—his lost love. He fought the desire to dress, hire a zombie-drawn rickshaw to take him to the Street of Flesh-Peddlers, to see her again, lying in her sealed glass casket. If only he had that money now he could buy her back from the death slavers, resurrect her as she deserved.

That is that, he decided. Sir Gahout be damned, I am going north.

The necromancer began with a reply to Baron Breka's request. He set pen to papyrus. *I accepted the terms as sufficient, etc. etc.* Then he rang a bell.

The servant that appeared, despite Fauston owning over forty undead slaves, was a living man.

"Ramid! Deliver this letter to Baron Breka's man, a tall fellow with a scar over his left eye. He's staying at the Craven Skull." Fauston sealed the letter with hot wax and his signet ring, which bore two severed heads with interlacing tongues. He made sure his valet saw him press the envelope shut. Unlike the undead that served the mage, Ramid was curious beyond the bounds of good taste.

"Yes, master."

"And Ramid, tell him I will meet him at the Craven Skull tomorrow morning, before the cock crows."

"Very good, master."

HE TOLD himself he had many preparations to make. He did not have time to cross the city to the Street of Flesh-peddlers. Still the zombie-drawn vehicle brought him closer to that house where his darling slept. Wasted minutes later he drew the heavy knocker on Frech's door. A thunderous boom followed.

The door opened in a moment to show Frech's steward, a

small wiry man with a harelip. "What? What?"

"I would see her," was all Fauston offered.

"Master Fauston," the servant said, realizing the station of the intruder.

"Take me to her, Backmon."

"This way." The steward disappeared into the dark comfort of the house. Fauston knew the way and pressed past the servant to the underground chamber where a row of sixteen glass cases filled a large room. "The master will be with you *shortly*."

Fauston ignored the servant's implied threat and went to the third case on the left. Under a velvet cover was the pale visage of Rayahl. Tears formed in Fauston's eyes.

"Do you have the twenty-thousand?" asked a voice from the shadows.

"No."

"Then why do you come here?" Master Frech stepped into the dull light of the lamps. He was a tall, acerbic man with no hair. His lips were the color of liver and his eyes burned with a dull, black shine.

"I will have it soon."

"How soon?"

"I have contracted work in the North. It will pay enough—"

Frech thought with a long, bony finger to his lips. "Good. Let's hope no one buys her in the mean time."

"What? We had a private deal."

"Yes, but you forget. One year. I should think a job up North would take – hm – six months. That's two months too long."

"I will be back before the year is over."

"You say—" Frech left his words hanging in the air.

"And I say this as well, if you sell my beloved to anyone but me, you will rue the day."

"'Major words from a minor mage'," quoted the flesh-peddler.

"You mock me, sir. But think on it. If I return with thirty thousand and have nothing to spend it on. That's a lot of money I can dedicate to your misery."

"You make your point, Fauston. How about this then? An extension – two months for another ten thousand."

"But I—" Fauston realized his mistake at last. Now Frech knew how much he was making on the deal.

"Damn you, five thousand."

"Five then. But after the six months, the price will be double. Or she may have been sold. It is my right. She is my property."

Fauston scowled as he recalled how Frech had bought the young woman's corpse from the bereaved parents for a mere five hundred skels.

"You'll get your money. And on time."

"Perhaps I can be of service—"

"Forget it, Frech. I'm not going to tell you anymore. You'll not steal this job out from under me. Good night."

With a last gesture of dismissal, Fauston left the house. He slammed the door on the way out, after shoving Frech's manservant out of the way. Despite his heated exit, he still thought he heard laughter coming from behind the closed door.

THE ZOMBIE-CART took him home. Once there he opened a safe hidden behind a tile in the wall, removed a sack of gold coins. My last three hundred, he sighed. It should prove enough.

As the rickshaw pulled him towards the Street of Arcane Tomes, Fauston heard the song of the thanator once again. Another hour had passed. Soon it would be morning and he'd have to be at the Craven Skull Inn to meet with Baron Breka's man. Riin was a city that slept by day, so the store that Fauston headed for was open. An undead cat sat guard at the door, only moving away for mages powerful enough to dispel it. *Keeps the posers out*, the owner had told him.

Fauston saw the owner-operator of the shop dusting a stack of books with an ostrich plume. Old Kesush smiled a toothless grin at the young mage. "Let me guess, the *Liber Ostenquaya*?"

"No. Bigger."

"Bigger? You must have made a windfall. Death grapple?"

"No, just saved it up the old fashioned way."

"Hm." The old man frowned. Life in the book business had few entertainments so when a good story came along Kesush was all ears. Some of the mages would fabricate a tale of adventure and horror for the old man's sake, but the falsehoods soon showed through and he lost interest. Fauston had more respect for the old necromancer. Maybe his adventures in the North would prove worthy of re-telling?

"I want your *Arcani Diablieri*." He plopped the sack of coins on the counter to reinforce his serious intentions.

Kesush shook his head. "Sorry, I haven't got one."

"Come on, Kesush. I know you have connections."

"That title is illegal, and with good reason. Mixing the forces of life and death is a blasphemous business—"

"And you should know—Kablish Kesush'nman."

The old bookseller stood aghast. "How? That name—"

"My father recognized you from when he was boy. He told me—told me never to reveal the fact unless it was dire. I need that book."

"How much gold?"

"Three hundred. My last three hundred. I'm broke."

The old man considered, then waved Fauston to the back of the shop. "Wait here."

The mage took a seat on an old divan while his elder rummaged through an old storage closet used for onions. After an eternity he came back with a bundle wrapped in the skin of a snow cat.

"Here. It is the only copy I have ever owned. I kept it because one just never knows when stronger magic will be necessary. But at my age, it hardly matters."

Fauston took the bundle, hide and all. The entire package smelled horribly of stale onions and wet soil. The necromancer opened up the fur to see a large, heavy book, not remarkable in any way. "Thank you. I—"

"Don't thank me, boy. You'll be cursing me before too long, I imagine."

"I am taking this North."

"It is yours. You paid me fairly for it."

"Still, I thought you'd want to know. It won't be turning up with the Captain of the Black Guard and a death warrant."

"We'll see—we'll see." Kesush walked away, shaking his head but cradling the velvet bag with loving, bony fingers.

Yes, we'll see.

THE RICKSHAW pulled up to the Craven Skull with a lurch. Fauston got down, placed his last half-skel in the undead hand, which disappeared onto a liver-brown tongue and down into the stomach. Unlike most zombie servants, the rickshaw-pullers had enough intelligence to make sure those riding with them paid. It took a very fast client to dodge those cold hands or a very good thief to slit the belly for the fare money.

Fauston looked about the front entrance of The Craven Skull. No one stood waiting. Had Baron Breka's manservant departed without him? His steps into the inn spoke of his fear but slowed when he saw a tall man sitting at a table. It took Fauston a moment to notice the man was finishing his eggs and tea. The reason for this was an outlandish headdress made from a lion's skin that the man wore. After that Fauston noticed the large broadsword strapped to his back.

"Are you Baron Breka's man?" he asked just to be sure.

The man belched. "Yup. Name's Bradur."

"Fine, when do we depart?"

"Just as soon as I finish my breakfast."

"There was a little matter of a second payment." Fauston said it with a sidelong glance at the others in the inn.

"Later." Bradur ignored him, tearing into his last fried egg.

The necromancer grunted, walked to the front door and looked for Ramid. No sign of him yet but a young lad handed him a piece of vellum. On it was written: "Will met you at river. RM." Ramid's writing was atrocious but he got the idea across. Fauston frowned. Written on his best vellum, the stuff he used only for court documents or gifts. Wasteful, that Ramid. Still, he had agreed to go north with him. That was something.

A loud burp behind him told the mage that his escort was finally ready.

"Is your Worship ready?"

"You may call me 'Master Fauston'," the mage corrected.

"Anything you say, your Worship."

THE BAGGAGE was packed, the undead servants chained together and ready for the long walk to the land of Baron Breka. Ramid sat astride a mule, acting as zombie-wrangler, his wand, a willow switch, dangling from one hand. The zombies were usually no problem—they certainly weren't going to argue with their master—but they did need an occasional course correction otherwise they'd end up walking on the bottom of lake or pointlessly trying to scale a cliff face. Unlike living men, they had no logical thinking – any thinking for that matter—to keep them free of obstacles or fire.

The manservant swatted at flies with his other hand, while staring off down the riverbank. Two figures had appeared a long ways off and slowly grew to be his master and a tow-headed outlander. Uggh, thought Ramid. What a barbarian! The lion headdress and that straggly moustache. And the sunburnt face just screamed "Peasant!" The fashion in Riin had been for slender waists, hairless faces and a skin as white as a fish's belly. To insure against tanning, both the master and the servant wore wide-brimmed hats that would keep the sun well away from their cheeks and noses. The worst Ramid could imagine from this adventure was a tan. If only he knew better…

Once altogether the party consisted of three men, a dozen undead, four horses and a mule. Fauston could not take all of his zombies with him. He had left the majority to carry on with the labor of the manor, under the direction of his nephew. Blau was a lazy dog, even compared to Ramid, but at least he was family, being the son of Fauston's eldest sister. The necromancer sighed once then kicked his horse forward.

The first incident between their guide and Ramid occurred

almost immediately. The lion-skinned warrior pulled his mount alongside the mule-riding servant. "If you keep kicking that mule like that, she'll be dead before we get to Shan."

"It's the only way to get her to move," objected Ramid.

"See that horse cart ahead of you?"

"Yes?"

"Tie a carrot to the back bumper. Make sure your mule knows it there—only don't let her have it until we stop for the day. She'll move."

"Thanks," Ramid allowed slipping from his lips before he remembered whom he was talking to. "Of course he's good with mules," he scolded himself. "He's a barbarian!"

The second incident happened once the troop had pulled up beside a small lake for the night. Bradur showed up after the zombies finished with the unpacking. The Northerner had two fresh coneys in his hands.

"Your master told me I should give these to you," said Bradur, handing over the rabbits. "How will you cook them?"

Ramid smiled. "First I'll debone them, then simmer them in butter, onions and my secret recipe of spices. Finally I'll bake them in pastry."

Bradur looked unimpressed but didn't object. Later when dinner was served he was surprised at the taste. "Ramid, this is mighty fine eating."

Ramid gave him a look as if to say, "What else?"

"It tastes just like my old nana used to make. The old bitch never told nobody her recipe neither. Mighty fine."

Ramid's look changed from snide indifference to outrage. As good as a barbarian's fodder! He retired to bed without so much as word to the zombies who cleaned the dishes.

Bradur had a look of his own. Suspiciously, he eyed the undead cleaning the plates. While riding he had been able to ignore the zombies, but here in camp he could clearly see their unseeing eyes and dead gray faces.

"You don't admire my handiwork?" asked Fauston, a slight smirk on his face.

Bradur, unsure if he would offend, only shook his head. "Where I come from the dead do not walk."

"Where I come from," countered the mage, "everything is done by the unliving, the sowing, the digging, the hewing and carrying. They are like machines, nothing more."

"T'ain't natural."

"Is a plow natural to the earth? A mill to the grain? No. Both are devices that men use to put Nature to his will. No different here."

"I don't like it."

"No, perhaps not, but your master Breka does. Tell me about Shan."

"There's not much to tell – compared to a city. Still, it suits me better. Shan is a hundred acres of farmland surrounding a keep. Walls taller than two men, a ditch. It's enough to keep the Drebins out." Bradur smiled fondly, looking off at the imaginary lands of memory.

"And who are the Drebins?"

"Just farmers and warriors like us, though they live in Drebh, of course."

"And these Drebins raid your farms, attack your stronghold."

"As often as we do theirs. Or the Torns or the Relhins."

Fauston nodded. Villages with chieftains or barons. And Breka was making his move. With Fauston's help he would take Drebh, Torn and Relh and any other comers and make himself king. It had happened that way in Ghand only two hundred years before. It was the way of the Northerners. Being the farthest from the Lorca territories of the south, it was easiest to forget that ever-present danger of invasion. The Lorcas hadn't attacked the mainland in force in fifty years. Only when the gods had left the world had greater calamity followed. Civilization had crumbled, leaving nothing more than petty kings with barbarous manners. Oh well, Fauston sighed, he'd have to get used to it.

"You need not keep a watch tonight, Bradur," Fauston said, changing the subject.

"Why is that, your Worship?"

"The zombies have been instructed to attack anything that enters the camp, to kill anything larger than a rabbit. They'll start wailing—"

"If it's all the same to you, I'll keep an eye open. What if we should be attacked by Turls?"

"Turls?"

"Little people armed with thorn spikes and poisoned flint knives – just smaller than a rabbit."

With a nod to Bradur, Fauston also retired for the night.

THE NEXT three days followed a similar pattern. Bradur rousted the camp at sunrise. Ramid cooked and directed the undead. Fauston did little but ride his horse and study the *Arcanis Diablieri* in the seclusion of his tent. He did not fear that Ramid would see the book and cut his throat for its evil reputation. Bradur was obliviously illiterate. Fauston's concern was more for the fact that Ramid was an incurable gossip. An undead standing before his tent door, supposedly to safeguard his person, was sufficient to keep his privacy.

On the fourth day, Fauston's privacy was disturbed by Bradur's roar and the shrill cry of the zombie guards. The undead burst into flames as arrows rained down on the camp. Ramid took a bolt in the thigh as he watched fire arrows strike the undead, turning them into walking torches.

Fauston leapt from his tent after securing the *Arcanis Diablieri* in a secret hole he dug before he slept each night. The mage flew from his tent with his hands free, ready to cast charms at any attackers. Instead he saw Bradur fighting three assailants at once. Their arrows spent, the bandits launched themselves from the shadows, swords swinging.

The lion-skinned warrior met their charge, his own broadsword free from the scabbard. The long blade blocked an ax stroke, then disappeared in a blinding flash as Bradur spun, decapitating his attacker. His fellows dove at the man, now that his blade was busy, but their target was no longer there. Trading places with the dead man, their knives fell on their slain comrade. Before they realized it, Bradur had gutted his second man.

Fauston could see four more man-shapes coming from the dark bushes. They're ringing Bradur in and then his prowess would count for nothing. The mage raised his hand, spoke the Chant of Drig softly. Even as the body of the second man hit the ground, the corpse of the slain bandits moved with new energy.

Bradur cursed and leapt away as the headless corpse of the first bandit grabbed the third by the throat. The second dead man, trailing intestines, joined him.

The four newcomers ran past the dead men, avoiding Bradur, dodging the burning zombies that finally fell to a stop in the bushes. The thieves' eyes were for the horses that were tethered inside the camp. Ramid screamed nearby at the arrow protruding from his leg.

"Master, they are after our horses!"

A bandit noticed Ramid then, and leapt to finish him with his short sword.

Fauston stood frozen as the man swung a blade at his servant. Too late, the mage drew his own dagger and ran into the fray.

The bandit screamed his victory, but his voice changed to a cry of agony as Bradur's sword hacked through the man's arm. Another bandit stabbed at the warrior but Bradur blocked the lunge and returned with an upward cut that split the man's chin.

The last bandit chose the better part of valor and disappeared into the darkness.

"If they're anymore of them, they'll be back," Bradur said to Fauston. "We'd better break camp and make an early start, just to be safe."

Ramid said, "My leg, my leg," over and over.

"Quiet, Ramid. I will tend to you in a moment." Fauston spoke without even looking at him.

Bradur gave him a curious look as he inspected the arrow sticking from Ramid's leg. "Can you cure him—by magic, I mean?"

"No, I work only with the dead." A strange look passed between the master and the servant.

"What?" asked the swordsman, noting their expressions.

"It is forbidden," supplied Ramid, biting back the pain. "A deathmaster must never mix life with death. That is the black art."

Fauston did not say anything to this but continued to examine Ramid's injury.

"Leave the arrow in for now. We can cut it out later," said Bradur.

"Yes, you're right. Please do what you can for Ramid, while I replace our carriers."

Fauston took quick stock of his original twelve zombies. Only two remained. Six were burnt. The fire arrows of the bandits had ruined them completely. Four were missing. Perhaps they'd pick them up as they left.

The mage examined the bodies of the slain. Of the six, only four were useable. The decapitated man would not suffice, nor would the man with his guts on the ground. If Fauston had more time he might have sewn him up again. The headless body could be reanimated as long as the necromancer was able to see where it moved, as during the fight, but without a head it would prove a poor servant.

The spell was expensive but quick. He now had four new servants.

"Take down those tents," he directed. "Pack those dishes." The commands were simple and the work was quickly done.

Bradur helped the wounded Ramid onto his mule. From there Ramid was able to assist his master with the wrangling of the undead. In less than a half hour the camp was packed, including Fauston's secret book, and they were on the move, riding in the opposition direction to the fleeing bandit.

As they rode away, Ramid spoke to Bradur. "I wanted to thank you for saving my life—"

"Think nothing of it," laughed the Northerner. "I just wanted more of that rabbit."

TWO DAYS later Bradur came into camp after a scouting expedition. "They're about a half-day's ride from here. We aught to catch up to them tomorrow."

Ramid looked to his master to answer his question, "Who?"

"A caravan heading to Ghand. We would travel farther east than I like but it would be safer."

The following afternoon the travelers spotted the dust cloud from the caravan and its chain of a hundred zombies. The only horses were used by the wranglers who worked up and down the lines, looking for problems. The zombie gang was the most reliable of convoys, for only the lead zombie needed directions, as the stumbling followers would go wherever their leader went first. Each dead man could carry a pack holding up to a hundred pounds of merchandise. More valuable treasures could be stowed in the stomachs of certain carriers known only to the master of the caravan.

Bradur rode on ahead. He carried a message to the caravan master, offering his ability with arms and Fauston's powers of magic as fair trade for the security of the zombie line. Ramid wondered if his abilities as cook would be offered. He began thinking of dishes he could serve their host. He selected one then another, knowing he'd left his freshest spices in Riin.

Bradur rode back, his broad grin telling them all of his success.

"They'll be glad to have us, especially tonight for some of their undead need mending."

Fauston nodded. He'd expected the caravan master would try and milk him of his necromantic abilities. Still, it was a small price to pay...

"And I offered Ramid's best skills to—"

The servant looked up with a grin. He would get to make that Roteeshan Chicken with black bean sauce!

"—as zombie wrangler," finished Bradur with a slap on his back. Ramid almost fell off his mule.

"Why, of all the –"

"That's enough, Ramid. We must all do what we can. And you need to rest that leg." Fauston gave him a look that said there be no point in arguing further.

Towards nightfall, the trio with their handful of zombies met up with the tail of the caravan. Bradur did not stop though, knowing the master of caravan would be close to the front of the line. Zombie wranglers challenged them occasionally as they rode up and down the line inspecting their charges. Ramid noticed, since thick ropes connected the undead, the wranglers did not waste their time with directing the carriers but in securing the packs that occasionally fell open. The undead gave no notice to the valuables falling out between broken straps. This was the only real danger to watch for besides bandits.

Another half hour's ride brought them to the caravan master, a fat man named Heyst, who rode in a hoodah atop an elephant. The giant beast was the only one in the train, making it easy to locate. Two guards protected their master with horn bows.

It was Bradur who moved up first, introducing Fauston, then Ramid.

"Welcome, welcome," said Heyst. "'Let us be stronger together.'" It was the customary greeting, as well as the final signing of their contract. Fauston answered likewise.

"Come aboard, Master Fauston. Let us talk awhile."

Accepting the offer, Fauston ascended into the hoodah, taking a glass of wine from Heyst's own hand. Ramid and Bradur were dismissed to their new duties as well as old.

Ramid cursed under his breath as he took Fauston's zombies and began to tie them together in a chain that tomorrow would be added to the caravan's hundred. Until the line stopped for the evening, Ramid would have to tend his own, marching on a parallel line with the train.

Bradur rode his horse down the line, then quickly back. His eyes were not on backpacks but on the horizon where bandits and wild beasts might lurk. His broadsword rested in its scabbard on his back but it was only a matter of seconds for it to be drawn and working. He also had a bow and quarrel of arrows hanging on his saddle. Since the caravan was in open county this weapon was more likely to be used since any enemy would appear long before it attacked.

An hour later, as the sun pinked the horizon, the train came to a gradual halt. The zombie wranglers were expert at stopping this shuffling parade with the minimum of confusion. Some of the hundred fell or collided with those in front and men had to reload spilled merchandise.

It was only after the zombies had set up camp and Ramid had fed himself and Bradur that Fauston showed up. Ramid inquired what dishes the caravan master had served him for his supper. Only after Fauston assured him it was inferior to Ramid's excellent fare could he ask Bradur his own question.

"How many days will we have to ride with the train—before we turn north to Shan?"

"Three at the least. After we cross the Torning River—"

"Torning? Is that near Torn, the village you spoke of?"

"Yes. We will probably spend the night there."

Fauston wrinkled his brow. "But they are your enemies—"

Bradur laughed. "You will need to gain an understanding of Northern politics, Master Fauston. On the surface we are all 'brothers together', all in league against the Lorcas, or whatever comers you can imagine. But, in fact, we are all working our hardest to acquire the rocks beneath each other's feet." He laughed again.

"It is safe then?"

"Quite. They will not attack a Shanman. Not openly. They will be curious about you though. They'll want to know what Breka's playing at. And they won't be too fond of your – carriers."

"Disguises perhaps?"

"They'd see right through it. No, better to impress them with your lordly manners. If things should come to that." Bradur left it at that, a smirk on his face that Fauston did not entirely appreciate.

THE JOURNEY to the River Torning took four days, not three. Bad weather lashed the zombie train mercilessly. Ramid rode with the other wranglers, despite his injury. The road became so bad the hundred-long chain was broken into three smaller lengths. One of these was put in Ramid's charge, the third including Fauston's dozen.

On the fourth day the rain turned to snow. The caravan came to the junction of two rivers.

"The Augus," said Bradur. "The caravan will follow it east to Ghand. And warmer days."

"And us?" asked Ramid hopefully.

"North, along the Swepa." The barbarian pointed at the smaller river that was lost in the distant snowfall.

"Farewell," said Heyst the caravan-master to Fauston alone, giving him an arm-grasp of friendship in the Southern fashion. "We will miss you."

"And us, you," agreed Fauston. *"May we be stronger apart,"* he finished the traditional breaking of their contract.

"But not for long," added Heyst with genuine affection.

The master of the caravan rose up onto his elephant's hoodah with a wave and they were gone, the train continuing on its way east. Ramid looked north, the direction of his own path and shook his head. Snow, and more snow.

The next day was a trial for everyone. The cold weather affected the zombies as much as the living. The necromantically animated flesh froze, making limbs unpliable. All the zombies had lost most of their fingers before Bradur called the party to a halt. He built a huge bonfire and Ramid placed the undead at a safe distance all around it.

Fauston pulled Bradur aside. "Is it always this cold here? I doubt if my skills will be of any use to your master in such a land."

"That is for Breka to decide," was all Bradur offered, going back into the woods for more fuel. Ramid was no help, lurking by the fire, complaining of his injured leg.

The Northerner returned, bearing an armload of branches. He threw them on the fire, then spoke to Fauston. "Keep to the fire. I know this cold is not what you are used to. But you can help by keeping an eye on the sky. As long as the weather stays snowy, the fire may go unnoticed. But if the sky clears, we will have to douse the flames."

"I doubt that men are about in this gale," said Fauston. "Not even bandits."

"I wasn't thinking of men."

The necromancer said nothing, just nodded, moving closer to the fire.

The three men spent a rough night around the fire, dozing off and on, but always with an eye to the flames.

With morning light came an end to the snow. By midday the air had turned spring-like and snow melted everywhere. This was good for the zombies, who cared not if slush soaked their boots or drops of snow fell off branches and down their necks. Ramid ruined his best pair of calf-leather shoes and did nothing but complain about it all afternoon. His lamentations only ended when Bradur said, "There—the outskirts of Torn."

Torn proved to be a collection of twenty log cabins. At the center of town was a palisade of pointed timbers, inside the residence of the barons of Torn. Bradur pointed out the crow standard on the red flag.

"The inn is this way," he said after Fauston and Ramid had their fill of the majestic lords of Torn.

The inn was a large log structure with two floors and a balcony that wrapped the entire circumference of the building. The common room was loud with drinking and song. Bradur greeted one fellow after another as he made his way to the innkeeper. Everyone cheered the Northerner as a brother, except for a few women who looked at him in a most unsisterly way.

"You seem popular hereabouts," said Ramid.

Fauston was aware of many blue eyes examining the darker features of himself and Ramid. He remembered Bradur's advice and walked up to the innkeeper with his most arrogant manner, and demanded the best room in the inn.

"Yes, my lord," said the innkeeper, a tall blond man in an apron. "Of course."

"And my carriers, they will need –"

"I was just arranging that part," broke in Bradur. "They'll be in the old barn. Ramid and I will see to them immediately." Bradur bowed to Fauston as if he had commanded this action. In fact he was signaling the necromancer to silence.

Fauston nodded his understanding, allowing the innkeeper to show him up the stairs to the second best room. The necromancer made a fuss until he was situated in the best room, one with a bathroom and small balcony overlooking the front of the inn. The innkeeper would have charged him the best rate anyway so he might as well enjoy it.

Bradur returned with Ramid a little while later. The big Northerner smiled. "Ramid, you should stay here with your master – enjoy a bath, dress that wound – while I, ah, make sure the locals are informed of your greatness. Say nothing of your carriers or your business with Breka. I am going to weave a little magic of my own." And with that he left the Riinians to themselves.

Not that either complained. There was hot water, towels and wine imported from Sharl. Only the food was disappointing, stew with hard brown bread and dull cheese made from goat's milk.

Fauston curled up on his bed. He thought of Rayahl, his dead love so many leagues away in Riin. The necromancer had washed his hair, oiled it in the manner of his people, then dabbed rose water under his arms and through his beard. For the first time in a week he did not smell of wood smoke and mud. Rayahl had liked to play with his beard when it was freshly oiled. Soon you will again, my darling, he promised.

A loud bang on the other side of the wall broke his reverie. A harsh female laugh was followed by a scream of delight as some man worked her up against the wall. Fauston thought to knock his disapproval but when he heard Bradur's baritone say, "Here's how we ride'em in Shan," the necromancer just sighed. There'd be no peace in this room he realized, as the barbarian applied himself to the task of satisfying the barmaid. And for such an indecently long time too...

THE FIRST time Fauston knew something was amiss was the next morning. Bradur had not returned, and at first the necromancer thought the big Northerner was probably nestled away with a naked wench somewhere, sleeping off his drunk. It was only as the mid-day meal came and went that he began to worry. Ramid laughed at his unease.

"He's probably started on today's binge—and wenches."

"I don't think so, Ramid. Look around us." The two sat on a bench on the wide veranda of the inn. There were quiet men and women going about their work. "A drunk would stand out like a moustache on the King's courtesan." The necromancer gave his servant a conspiratorial look. "You have checked the barn?"

"Yes, master. The – uh – carriers are fine."

"Damn that barbarian. If he's gotten himself killed I'll resurrect him just so I can kill him again."

Ramid did not smile at the jest. He knew what his master's powers were capable of.

"Come on, Ramid. Let's go find him."

"But how, master?"

"Look for something out of place."

"But everything is out of place here. No zom—I mean carriers—to do the work."

"Still, look around."

The two Riinians walked about the streets of Torn, the tall master and his limping servant with a crutch of oak wood, gathering the occasional glance from locals but little else. The entire tour took only ten minutes since the village had only five short avenues.

Ramid pointed out a couple washing a pig.

"That's unusual, master."

"They like their swine clean hereabouts, Ramid. I hardly

think it is sinister."

"No, master."

Ramid pointed out a horse next, its mane braided in the worst barbarian fashion.

"See, master? There by that barn where all those people are going."

"You miss the warts for the toad. The horse is ugly to be sure but unimportant. But that barn—"

"Surely these people go into barns, master."

"Yes, but not usually all at the same time. Let's go."

The two men approached what was a ramshackle shed of weathered planks. The sound of shouted excitement inside pounded out the empty doorway. Ramid walked behind his master like a reluctant child, for inside the barn was a circle of Tornians all watching and cheering. No one challenged them as they joined the ring.

In the middle of the circle was not a cockfight as Ramid expected, though such fights in Riin did not use live animals but reanimated ones. Instead he saw Bradur stripped to the waist, bound and held by two Tornians. His lion-skin headdress was also gone, so Ramid did not recognize him immediately. Another man, a tall thin man with raven-black hair held a red-hot branding iron in one hand. The crowd cheered as he approached Bradur, who fought hopelessly with the two men who held him.

Ramid was confused when his master pulled him stealthily out of the ring of spectators. A short distance away Fauston stopped, whispering instructions to his servant. "Quickly," he finished. "And don't forget the black case under my bed!"

With that Ramid exited the barn in the direction of the inn.

"This is how we brand Shanmen here in Torn," shouted the raven-haired man, the brand now only inches from Bradur's face.

"Stop!" cried Fauston in his most commanding voice. "Do not hurt this man. He is my servant."

"Go away, city-man. This is Northern business," swore the man with the iron.

The spectators moved away from Fauston, allowing him to enter the theater of their little drama.

"How can you say it does not concern me? If this man is injured he will not be able to administer to his chores."

"Too bad. Find another guide. He slept with my wife."

"Terrible, but to maim a man for it?"

"He's been warned *before*."

"And all your children have yellow hair!" laughed a man from the circle. Everyone joined him except those involved.

"I'll kill him!" yelled the raven-haired man.

"Stop! Or else—" Fauston raised his hands in a dramatic way, a magical charm dangling from his fingers. In truth the chain was nothing more than one of Ramid's over-extravagant tassels used for tying up dishtowels.

"Or what?"

"Or you will regret it!"

The crowd forgot Bradur as their attention shifted from the bound man to the newcomer. "Derog! Derog!" they chanted to the raven-haired man.

Derog smiled viciously as he took a swipe at Fauston's head. The necromancer ducked then backed towards the barn door.

"I warned you. Do not forget that."

Derog dove at him but fell back when dark forms came through the barn door. Ten lumbering shapes came from the bright exterior into the dimmer shades. Derog plucked up his courage and slammed the branding iron into the face of his new opponents. He screamed when he saw that the iron did nothing to a neck that already hung broken. Cold, fish-white hands reached past his swing and clamped around his throat. He squealed as the dead hands crushed his windpipe, maggots cascading all over him in the process.

Then things seemed to explode inside the barn. Undead forms collided with the living and someone, alive or dead, knocked over the hot coals with which Derog heated his branding iron. The flames and smoke quickly drove out those who had not already fled.

Fauston reached Bradur's slumped form with two quick strides. He helped the barbarian to his feet and headed past his army of undead soldiers.

"Come on, wake up, Bradur! Ramid has gone for the horses. We are leaving Torn."

"Good. 'I've stayed one wench and a dozen ale too long', as my daddy always said."

"Shut up and run."

FAUSTON BEGAN to press his horse into a fast trot when he reined in suddenly. Ramid saw him stop and turned and looked. Bradur, instead of being behind him, was galloping away, back towards the burning barn.

"Master, why?"

"I have no idea, Ramid. These Northerners are all crazy."

After a moment, Fauston turned back to the north and rode at a steady clip.

A half hour later the two men heard hooves thundering in their direction. A second later Bradur pulled up, his head bearing a slightly burnt lion headdress.

"You went back for that – thing?" said Ramid, not bothering to hide his disgust.

"Yes. You didn't think I'd leave you gents now? We're almost in Shan."

Fauston said nothing. He didn't think he could reply without breaking into a grin. And he'd never give this barbarian servant the satisfaction of that response.

They rode on in silence. Finally Ramid asked what both of the Southerners were wondering, "Where'd you get that thing anyway?"

"From my father. His father ventured into the Southlands, after the Lorcas were repelled. He killed this cat with only a dagger. Bore the scars the rest of his years."

"But surely, it wasn't worth going back into that barn for?"

"My father lost it once in a game of dice. He rode all the way to Ghand to get it back. Surely, that barn was nothing compared to that."

Ramid eyed him, suspicious that the Northerner was mocking him. He gave his master a look that agreed with his earlier assessment. Crazy.

"Is it far to Shan from here?" asked Fauston, trying to change the subject.

"Not far. If we ride until dark, then camp for the night, we should be eating lunch in Shan tomorrow."

"Good. I tire of Tornian hospitality."

Ramid said nothing to this, still thinking of Bradur's comments. Was it really some romantic family heirloom? Or was it the bald spot he's seen on Bradur's head when they had him tied up? The servant grinned slyly to himself.

"Onward!" cried Bradur, kicking his horse to speed. "On to Shan and some real Northern Hospitality, worthy of a prince!"

Fauston followed suit but he only wanted to be back in Riin, back with his Rayahl, back in a decent, sensible world where he was master of life and death.

Lastly came Ramid. He looked once more at the smoke from the direction of Torn, then ahead to the stark trees and distant hills. What lay ahead for them in Shan? Only the gods knew, he thought, and the gods have left us to find out for ourselves.

Part Two: The Leash

"It is easier to bind a dog with meat than rope."
– Northern proverb

FAUSTON DID not see Baron Breka for two days after arriving in Shan. The necromancer and his servant were installed in a cabin of sawed logs, ate in the communal hall and waited on their master's bidding.

This gave the newcomers a chance to get to know Shan and all its lack of marvels. A dirt road separated the small city into two. On one side a half circle of log structures, a few even of two storeys. On the other side the community hall, the Baron's headquarters, the parade ground where warriors drilled in the evenings by executive order. Only the ill, the wounded and the dead were exempt. Beyond the training grounds were the slaughter yard, the refuse dump and beside that, the guest quarters which included Fauston's little cabin.

"Master, the Baron does you an insult placing us here," said Ramid, surly with dark rings around his eyes. His bed was a sack filled with straw placed over boards. Even his camping bedding was better.

"Nonsense, Ramid. The Baron is actually a pretty smart fellow. The winds that blow through here are always from the north. The stench of the garbage piles blows away from us." Fauston yawned. He had been catching up on his sleep and had even managed to feel full for a change. The journey from Riin had taken weeks, fraught with dangers that had taxed his energies.

"I'm going back to bed," sighed the servant. "Wake me if an incredibly beautiful woman calls or someone shows up with a decent pillow."

Ramid had finally made himself comfortable when a loud knock echoed through the cabin. Fauston opened the door himself to see Bradur's leonine headdress and a big grin.

"The Baron has requested your presence."

"Finally," said Ramid throwing off his simple blankets.

"When does he wish to have his audience?" asked Fauston. "Tonight? Tomorrow?"

"Now."

"Now!" squealed Ramid. "But the master will need to dress and prepare. I couldn't have him ready in less than two hours."

"Now, and don't make him wait. It makes him grumpy." Bradur crossed his massive arms and leaned against the doorframe impatiently.

"There's no time, Ramid. Bring me my bag, and my best robe. I can wear that at least, can't I?" He asked this of Bradur.

The swordsman just shrugged his shoulders. *Do as you*

please.

Robe pulled over his nightclothes, Fauston followed Bradur, with Ramid bringing up the rear and the bag. They walked around the refuse dump in the direction of the Baron's headquarters. The Riinians could see the stripped bones of cattle, pigs and oxen. Fauston recognized the large piles as preparations for war. Meat for troops. He imagined somewhere else men were forging weapons, fletching arrows and building barrels for storage. It was the first time Fauston truly realized he was entering a war zone.

Bradur acknowledged a soldier posted on guard at the front door as they approached the large square building that served as Breka's headquarters. The spearman thumped his weapon in salute as he allowed the three to enter. Once inside, it took a minute for their eyes to adjust to the dimmer light. Two oil lamps, evenly spaced, burned on a table in a room that took up most of the entire structure. Around this table stood three men.

"Ah, you've brought me my sorcerer at last, Bradur," said the largest of the big warriors, each dressed in fur tunics with cloth trousers. Each bore a collection of gold rings, torcs and armbands. Only the man who spoke wore a circlet of gold on his shaggy head.

Bradur bowed to his liege-lord, then introduced their guests. "Baron, I am pleased to introduce Fauston, necromancer of Riin, and his man, Ramid."

"Come, come, join us, Fauston. We are discussing our attack on Drebh. I believe we will have our first chance to use your services here." The Baron waved his hand over a large map that the men pointed at with their daggers.

"Greetings, my lord," said Fauston nervously. "I would happily discuss strategy with you but there is a little matter of our arrangement that needs to be completed first."

The Baron laughed. He slapped Bradur on the back. "You never told me these magicians were so mercenary, Bradur. I like him already."

"Nor I, Baron," answered Bradur, flashing Fauston a dark

look.

"Alright, Fauston *magister,* let's conclude our business first. You say you can raise the dead, make them do your bidding. Let us see. Gorn, Luerc." At this the two men who stood with the General leapt with effortless speed and power. They had Ramid between them in an instant. The Baron stepped forward with his dagger in one ham-sized fist. "I will slice up your pet, and we'll see how well you can patch him back together."

"Baron," interceded Bradur quickly. "I have seen this magic done. There is no need to harm this servant."

"Sit down, General, or you'll take his place."

Bradur drew his own blade. "I can not allow this, my lord. This man owes me a blood debt. I would see that he completes his service to me."

"Forget it, Bradur. I will give you gold instead."

"No, my liege."

"Whores, then."

"No, it is a matter of honor."

The Baron looked at the General then nodded to Gorn and Luerc. The two men let Ramid go. The Riinian collapsed in a pile at their feet.

"What good are sorcerers if we have to treat them like virgins?" demanded Gorn.

"I admit they are not the most fearsome of creatures," said Bradur sheathing his knife. "But they have their uses. Do we still have that Drebhian spy?"

The Baron laughed. "Yes, of course, I was going to kill him as soon as we finished here. Go get him, Gorn."

The warrior Gorn left and returned in a minute with what once had been a man. The torturers had beaten him to a shade of purple. Fauston was amazed he was still alive, then he recalled the strength and vitality of these Northerners.

"Hayten, I have something special for you. This man here is a wizard of great renown. He's going to give you second chance to be useful to Shan." The Baron laughed at his own simple joke before he shoved his dagger into the man's belly. Hayten coughed up blood, thrashed in Gorn's arms and then expired with curses mixed in with the blood bubbles.

"How damaged can he be before it doesn't work?" asked the Baron coldly as if he hadn't just killed a man.

"A-ah, quite a bit," answered Fauston. "As long as the bones, tendons and muscles remain, the rest doesn't really matter."

The Baron grabbed the dead man's hair, drew up his chin. He slashed his blade across the throat, adding more blood to the floor. He did the same to the exposed meat of the man's thighs. "That should do. Magister?" Gorn let go of the corpse, allowing it to fall roughly on its face.

"Ramid, bring me my bag."

Ramid complied, happy to have something to do. Fauston extracted a large leather pouch. He sprinkled some dust over the body, then quietly to himself spoke the chant that activated the magic.

"Rise!" Fauston said in a loud voice that even made the Baron jump. The ruler of Shan might have said something in retaliation but his mouth hung open as Hayten stood up, his head rolling back and forth with the effort.

"Kill!" said Fauston pointing at the Baron.

The undead spun to its right and threw still warm fingers about the Baron's throat.

"Stop!" cried the necromancer as he saw Gorn and Luerc raising their knives. "Kill them!" Fauston pointed at the knifemen. Hayten spun without any further notice of the Baron and stumbled into Gorn and his descending blade. The zombie took the knife without notice, then shoved Gorn into his companion.

"Stop!" Fauston said again. The creature did as commanded.

Laughter was the next thing the necromancer heard. Breka was slapping his thighs and hooting at his friends. "Enough, sorcerer. Enough."

"Should we kill him?" asked Gorn, nodded at Fauston, hoping to do the task.

"How could you, Gorn? That zombie would stop you,"

answered the Baron. "No, no, we asked for a demonstration and we got one." To show that he had no hard feelings the Baron slapped Fauston on the back with a blow even Bradur couldn't match. "But fetch my sword, Luerc."

The warrior left without question, returning with the Baron's three and a half foot long broadsword. The blade was wider than most swordsmen preferred but Breka's massive arms found no trouble wielding the sinister weapon. The Baron unsheathed it, throwing the scabbard onto the table.

"Try it again, sorcerer. I would see how long one of these fellows last once created."

"As you wish." Fauston pointed at the Baron and gave the command to kill. The zombie stepped forward immediately.

The Baron raised his sword and swung, hacking off an arm. The zombie jerked but came on all the same. The Baron's second swing would have gutted a living man. Hayten's intestines poured out but the undead man came on. A third swing and the head followed the arm. This time the corpse didn't even hesitate but reached the Baron with its good hand.

"Stop!" commanded Fauston.

"No need, sorcerer," said the Baron raising the weapon a last time and striking a heavy blow at the headless neck. The blade cut deep into the trunk, almost hacking the zombie in two. The undead creature collapsed, finally destroyed.

More laughing. The Baron smiled widely as he cleaned his sword and resheathed it. "Good. This is good, Bradur. An army of these along with living men and who can stop us."

"Yes, Baron. Though I think maybe you've hit the nail on the head there." Bradur looked at his feet as he said this.

"What?" demanded Breka.

"Will our men fight alongside their own dead?"

"I leave that to you, Bradur. Take some men, take the sorcerer and figure it out. Let me know in three days."

"Yes, my lord." And with that the interview was over. Bradur lead the two Riinians outside. There were no more offers to discuss strategy.

"Damn, that was a close one, your worship," said the General as they walked the single street of Shan, back toward the guesthouses.

"Close?" asked Fauston.

"Yes, your quailing will be the death of you. Only strength is respected here. But you came through in the end. That was a stroke of genius to attack the Baron."

"Not genius, just pique. I don't like being shoved anymore than you do."

"Good, good. Keep that in your heart."

"What about me? I almost died in there," growled Ramid.

"We all 'almost died in there', Ramid. But your master saved us all so we can die in three days."

"What?"

"If we fail, all three of us will be thrown on spears. Or worse."

"Why should we fail?" asked Fauston.

"You may know magic, your worship, but I know fighting men. But let's worry about that tomorrow." Bradur's whole demeanor changed instantly. "I've got a hankering for a few ales and a good roll in the sack before I die. Meet you here in the morning." With that he was gone in the direction of a house where the women were more generous than the wine cups.

THE MORNING proved to be drizzling and wet. Fifty men stood on the parade ground in full battle armor, leather and iron with helmets of bronze. Each bore a spear, a sword and a shield. And a frown that could curdle cream.

"Alright, you pissants. Today you're going to kill Drebhans. You should be smiling, assholes." Bradur showed them his wide grin. "And to make it even easier for you, I have something special."

"A raincoat would be nice," said one wiseacre in the back.

"I know that was you, Boreen. I'll deal with you later. Now listen up, you sons of whores. These necklaces are special magic." Bradur held up one of the fifty-one bags Fauston and

Ramid had made all afternoon the day before. "See, I'm putting mine on, because I want extra protection from Drebhans. I will be invincible. I will be alive come the morrow so I can brag about all the heads I smashed. Now, get in line, and put them on."

The soldiers took the amulet bags and did as instructed. They were a surly lot, unhappy to be out in the rain, but they were also superstitious. Anything that helped keep you alive in battle was welcome.

For the rest of the morning they walked. The border between Shan and Drebh was only ten miles away, their rivals being a village much like Shan. Bradur knew there would be sheep and cattle grazing on a hillside just on the other side of the Shan territory. Twenty to thirty soldiers were all that was needed to guard this rich grassland. Bradur's orders were to take as many cows as possible, and kill as many Drebhans as possible. The cattle would be slaughtered and their meat saved for Breka's coming campaign.

"Fifty men seems a large number for a cattle raid," said Ramid to Bradur when he had a moment alone with him.

"Yes, but there's something else."

"Something else?"

"You'll see."

And Ramid did as they passed a set of markers, poles bearing skulls. "This is the end of Shanian land. We're in Drebhan territory now." Beyond the markers, Ramid could make out a natural narrowing of the mountains and boulders scattered about.

"There," said Bradur. "That's 'The Devil's Arshole'. Though I've heard Drebhans call it the 'Baron's Sphincter'."

"What is it?"

"A narrow spot before the valley opens up into grassy slopes. It's there the Drebhans post guards. Five Drebhans can hold back fifty men from that spot alone."

"Arrows?"

"No good. We have to go through there and it will cost us men."

"And the men will go?"

"Sure. The first man through gets his pick of the cows, horses if we're lucky. Whatever. And bragging rights."

The servant just nodded and for the thousandth time realized that Northerners were all madmen.

The fifty men stopped at Bradur's whispered command. "Everybody got their amulet?" The general lost a few minutes getting pouches in place. One warrior had gambled his away to another who now wore two. A third had opened his and emptied it into his pocket. A nod from Fauston told Bradur it didn't matter. It worked as well from a pocket as a pouch.

"Here's the plan. Forgus, Gwino, you're been here before, you'll remember. We use the boulders to sneak as close as we can, then on my word we all charge. First man through gets the choicest prize." This last part drew grins of avarice from mouths missing teeth.

"What's the foreigner going to do?" asked one fellow named Vins. He pointed at Fauston.

"He is a sorcerer. He is going to cast another spell over us all, to make the Drebhans wish they'd stayed in bed."

A quiet laugh and they began moving out, crouching as they worked their way from boulder to boulder. A cry came up from the Devil's Arsehole as the Shanians were spotted. Ramid could make out three guards armed with bows. An arrow shot out from the rocks, missed, splintering against a boulder.

When the majority of the fifty had found their way to the last set of rocks, Bradur gave the signal to charge, a crow's caw. In a group the warriors left the shelter of the boulders and ran toward the Drebhans, voices raised in war cries. Bradur was not one to lead from the rear, being the second or third man into the press. The front man fell, three arrows in his chest. Missiles flew over Bradur's head as he brought his sword up and into action. He cleaved a Drebhan archer through the neck, cutting his weapon in two at the same time.

More men fell but the Shanians were quickly establishing themselves at the neck of the barricade. The first man through was the man next to Bradur. He cheered at his good luck then fell dead with a spear through his guts. More Drebhans arrived, reinforcing their fellow guards. Bradur raised his sword in signal. Now, realized Fauston. The necromancer threw some of the mystic dust into the air and intoned his arcane words.

The warriors of Shan were using swords, their spears gone. They did not at first notice the dead men rising from the ground behind them. Even as these stumbled through the gap and engaged their foes they did not recognize what nature of men they were. It was only as they saw brothers and cousins who had been alive a moment before, saw them cut down then rise again, did it come home. The Drebhans also saw the dead reaching and grasping for them, and fled screaming. The Shanians cried out and fled back through the gap. Bradur's shout to press the attack was ignored as the men fled back towards the boulders.

The General cursed then hurried back through the gap to find Fauston on top of a boulder. Bradur arrived in time to see the men pulling off their amulets and preparing to charge Fauston from all three sides. "Come down, wizard and we'll deal with you," shouted the swordsman named Vins.

"Stand down!" Bradur yelled.

"This foreigner has cursed our dead. We would kill him now."

"Stand down. The foreigners do this thing with the Baron's blessing. Forget them. The Drebhans have run away like a bunch of girls. Their cows eat grass just over the hill. Gather as many as you can. Go!"

The warriors looked at each other, then at Fauston then did as they were told. They spit curses at the necromancer as they walked away.

"You foresaw this, Bradur?" asked Fauston who had not moved from his gloomy perch.

"Yes. Still, we've won the day here. Breka will be happy with a few cows. But we have work to do. When the cowards get back to Shan they will have blown up this tale to a veritable invasion of corpses. They will have painted you so black I fear none will wear these charms." With that, Bradur pulled off his own necklace and threw it away.

ALL OF Bradur's predictions had come true. Men armed with spears waited for the Riinians as they walked back with the remains of Bradur's squad. The booty of fourteen cows and two horses did little to calm their fears. The General's blade and threats could hold them only so long. It took the Baron's own appearance and threat of terrible death to dispel them. He finished with, "Bradur, bring them here."

Once more in the war room, Breka looked at Fauston and Breka in even turns. "Not the success I had hoped for."

"No, my lord."

"What do we do now, *magister*?"

Fauston was about to say his magics worked fine, the problem was with the men, but decided on silence instead.

The Baron stared down at his map table. "In two-score days we march on Drebh. I need this matter solved immediately. Understand?"

"Yes, my lord," Bradur said looking at his feet.

Breka left. Fauston turned to the General. "What do we do?"

"I know not. I think in three days we'll be feeding the crows."

It was Ramid who spoke next. "Master, I can't say I understand these Northerners, but this does remind me of a time in my dance school."

"Dance school?" bellowed Bradur. "What nonsense is this? We are dealing with men, not traipsing capons."

"Be quiet, Ramid. We need to think."

"But master, I think I have solved this. If you'll hear me out."

In a whisper, Fauston said, "No more about dancing. Let's call it 'sword practice'."

"Alright, during my time in 'sword practice school', there was an incident when all the danc—swordsmen would not practice with one partner, a girl named Prinzett, who had huge feet, pimples and a distinct body odor – I think she had Northerner blood— but that doesn't matter."

"Yes," sighed Fauston, rolling his eyes.

"Well, the danc—sword master solved this by getting a really big necklace, with a flashy gem."

"Now we are discussing gewgaws?"

"Patience, Bradur," interceded Fauston. "Go on."

"The swordmaster said this jewel could only be worn by one accomplished enough to dance with Prinzett. He told his best student he was not worthy, giving it to his second best. The competition between these two, and later all the others had Prinzett so busy she finally quit the school, claiming sore feet."

"So, you are suggesting we make the pouches an honor?"

"I think I begin to see," grinned Bradur, "Only we won't use pouches, we'll use something new, flashier. The others, who have to win their spurs, will wear the pouches."

"I would suggest you start with the men who came back with us today. A ceremony to present them with their new honor. And a title, the Baron's Gentlemen, or something."

"You're brilliant, Ramid," admitted Bradur. "But I think this needs a Northerner touch. The Baron's Bloodguard. Yes, that'll do the trick. Let's go. The sooner, the better. Rumors will be burning through town. We need to stem them as soon as possible."

AND SO the Bloodguard was created, and Breka smiled again as his army was readied for the assault on Drebh. Not every man wore the pouch but well over half wanted the honor of the gold necklace that went with the title. The necklaces had come from Bradur's private stash but he didn't begrudge the cost. He was too fond of living.

In a private moment, Ramid whispered to his master. "Those necklaces—"

"Yes, Ramid, they're from the Temple of Harkusa. I recognized the Harkusi too."

"But whore necklaces?"

"They have skulls on them. And these Shanians know them not."

"Well, most of the Shanians. Bradur seems to own a lot of them."

"Well, he has been traveling to Riin frequently on the Baron's business."

Ramid said no more about the trinkets that the priestesses of Harkusa gave to their supplicants after making their sacrifices of a sexual nature.

Fauston couldn't have discussed it with Bradur anyway. The General left soon after on another of his missions for the Baron.

"I hope to be back in time for the attack," he told Fauston as he mounted his black mare. "Keep out of trouble while I'm gone, will you?"

"Come back quickly," was all the necromancer said.

THE INCIDENT Bradur warned Fauston against came on the seventh day after he left. The necromancer and his servant had fallen into a dull routine of late breakfast, an afternoon of work filling and charming amulet pouches and then watching the nightly drilling of the warriors. Fauston could not help but smirk at the exalted position the 'Baron's Bloodguard' had attained. Though not exempt from practice, they lorded their status over their fellows mercilessly. The necromancer could feel the growing impatience of the others to win this same rank.

The incident wasn't with the warriors, as Bradur had worried. It came in the guise of an old woman. The two men did not notice her at first as they watched the spearmen practice lunging at imaginary enemies. The old crone was standing beside Fauston before he could stop her.

"*Nargesh,*" the old voice cursed before running her arthritic talons across the necromancer's face. "Nargesh!" she screamed loud enough to turn heads on the practice field. Officer and soldier stopped, leaned on their spears to watch.

"Get away, old one!" said Fauston, pressing her away with care.

"*Nargesh, suli meccek*!" she babbled through toothless gums.

"Begone!" said Ramid, finally coming to his master's rescue.

"Please, leave me alone!" barked Fauston, trying to free himself of her claws.

Laughter from the soldiers sprinkled the air. No one made any move to stop the old hag.

Finally, Ramid had her off his master, allowing Fauston to flee with his bleeding cheek. The servant let go off the woman only after she spit in his face. She hobbled off in the opposite direction.

A smiling officer asked Ramid, "Are you alright, city-man, or should we fetch the surgeon?" His charges laughed.

"What was she saying?" asked Ramid, ignoring the jibe. "What is *Nargesh*?"

"It means 'cursed one'."

"Our magic has frightened her."

"I think not. Old Nilli is a witch herself. Says she can raise the dead too."

"Professional jealousy then?"

"No, she is a Meoi. They're half-Lorcan some say. Breka tolerates them but they are no friends to Shan. Or Drebh, or anyone."

"The Baron should send her away. Why doesn't he?"

"Like I said. He tolerates her."

"Why?"

"Because she is very good at spotting demons."

Ramid said nothing to this, but his brow was furrowed with dark worries.

AFTER THE encounter with the witch, Fauston and Ramid did not leave the area of the guest cabins unless invited by the Baron. He did this on a number of occasions with questions about the undead warriors. How long would they march? Did they have to be fed? How would they be disposed of after the battle? Fauston answered all these with good detail and the Baron slapped him on the back only when the necromancer wasn't quick enough to place a table between them.

"Tomorrow we attack, *magister.* Are the pouches ready?"

"One thousand, and a few hundred spares."

"Good. The men keep asking for them. Bradur did well."

Fauston just nodded, then asked about the General. "Will he be back soon? In time for the assault?"

"I know not. He is overdue. But he travels far on very little time, so we will have to wait and see." With those words the Baron dismissed him, moving back to his map table and conferring with his lieutenants.

The morning brought cold sunshine and a thousand warriors standing at attention on the practice field. Fauston could see ten centuries of infantry, a mere fifty cavalrymen, each with a horse barded in armor. The Shanians did not use separate archers but each tenth man carried a quiver and short bow instead of a spear. These hundred men would fire in a group before the assault began, then discard their bows for swords. None as yet wore the pouches that would resurrect the dead.

The necromancer and his servant, with the help of two blond Shanians, had the thousand necklaces in three barrels. A century at a time the warriors lined up for these, some shaking them gleefully or kissing them before putting them on. Only the Bloodguard and the horsemen did not receive them. The Bloodguard had already won their metals, while a zombie horseman was not an idea Fauston even wanted to consider.

"Will this ever begin?" asked Ramid, who blew on his cold hands and juggled his master's bag of magical components.

"The scouts have already left," said Fauston. "We follow any time. You and I have been given permission to ride in the baggage train."

"Good."

"Not good. We won't be riding, to arrive hours after we are needed. No, we march with the men."

Ramid frowned but knew better than to argue the point.

"There's the bugler's call. Ready?" asked the master.

"I wish Bradur was here," Ramid answered, changing the subject.

"So do I. But the Baron is leading this assault himself. Bradur would be over there with the cavalry."

"Yes, but I'd feel better all the same."

"Shut up and start walking."

THE TWO Riinians said little before arriving at the Devil's Arsehole. Scouts and advanced troops had arrived an hour before and the arrows were all spent. A few dead Drebhs decorated the gap between the boulders and the Drebhan lands beyond. A few Shanians had also fallen but Fauston realized it was too soon to activate his charms. Was he to wait for Breka's instructions or decide for himself when to strike? The answer for that came in the form of Gorn. The huge lieutenant stood with his thumbs in his sword-belt.

"His Lordship has sent me to tell you that you must wait until you hear his horn blast three times. Only then are you to raise the dead." He said all this with obvious distaste.

"Understood. Three blasts."

The lieutenant turned and left without saying another word. Fauston had noticed that he wore no pouch at his neck.

The necromancer and his man sat on a large rock and watched the minor skirmishes the Shanians made against the rocks. The arrows flew no more from either direction. Spears were raised and the battle horns of Shan blew once in a long whining drawl. The foot soldiers raised their shields in a line and began marching toward the gap.

The advantage was all on Breka's side. The Drebhans knew they couldn't defeat an army here, but the men who held the position bought time for the rest of Drebh to gather arms for a clash that would take place elsewhere. In a matter of minutes the gap was taken and Shan marched on Drebh. The last of the defenders either died or fled as consciences dictated.

"Time to go," said Fauston, getting up off his rock.

The line moved through the gap and the two Riinians squeezed in through between two centuries of soldiers. The grasslands beyond the rocks were green and bare of cattle. Fauston did not ask where to go as the file of tramping figures was evident, running from the gap down to a stream covered in willows and cottonwoods. There the dirt trail became a full-fledged road. The Shanians marched on in the dust. Birds sang from the green leaves making the dull thump of booted feet seem oddly incongruous.

The Drebhans knew their territory well and had picked a large stone bridge across the stream—now swollen to a boulder-filled river—to place their quickly gathering line. Four hundred warriors stood with spear and shield at the far end of the bridge. Their numbers grew with every minute. Breka planned to press his advantage of numbers and attack immediately.

Fauston leaned against a large poplar and spied out the lay of the land and the dispersal of Breka's men. A century of spearmen held the bank on their side of the bridge, while the rest sat behind them, along the road in orderly groups. Of the cavalry he could see nothing. They were either kept in hiding or attempting to cross the river elsewhere. A few scouts were testing the waters of the river but the depth and speed soon curtailed this. A few arrows also sent the men back to the bosom of their army.

The horns called again. A century of soldiers was arranged to assault the bridge. This honor of going first had been settled back in Shan when the leaders of each cohort had drawn straws in a lottery. Not a lottery of dread, but one of expectation, for each man wanted his squad to be first over the bridge. The lucky winners prepared their shield wall, which was only four men wide for this was all the bridge width allowed, their spears pointed eagerly outward.

Another call and the century went forward with a trained deliberation that surprised Fauston. He had expected something less organized, more savage. As the first squad left, the second took up position behind them, waiting for their call to attack. But the necromancer wasn't watching these men but the first, who crashed into the Drebhans with a noise that could be heard all the way on the other side of the river.

Slaughter. That was what it was. To a man the first line fell.

The second were not far behind and they too crashed, dying everywhere. A third hundred fell in behind and the defenders were now feeling the sharp edge of the sword, for the Shanians almost broke the line except for a squad of fifty who reinforced the Drebhans, who now numbered at least six hundred.

The Shanians fell back at another long whining call of the horn. They retreated to the middle of the bridge, pressing themselves against the railings. Ramid asked his master, "What are they doing?"

"I don't know. Wait and see."

"Maybe we won't even be called today."

"Wait and see."

Fauston turned at the sound of horses' hooves. The cavalry came from behind a knoll and took up their position at the head of the bridge. A warrior who Fauston recognized as Bradur's second-in-command, raised his sword and in a group the horsemen began to charge across the bridge. The animals gathered speed quickly, running over one warrior too slow to press himself against the rail, and crashing into the Drebhan pikemen who hurriedly assembled themselves on the far side.

Ramid looked away as horses screamed and lances splintered. He did not see the next squad of warriors who followed the horsemen, to take advantage of the crushing blow of the cavalry. For a long moment it looked as if the Drebhans were going to flee, but they only fell back ten yards and took up a new position. This elbowroom allowed the Drebhan cavalry to ride in from their hiding place behind a number of outbuildings, slamming into the Shanians flank. The attackers faltered, fleeing back onto the bridge where the cavalry did not follow. But this move had cut off a small group of attackers who had gathered around the Shanian horsemen, now surrounded they were being cut down like stocks of wheat from all directions.

The horns blew again and more Shanians ran across the bridge to bolster their comrades. But the Drebhans had foreseen this move and had thrown bails of oil-soaked hay onto the bridge and lit them. The fire barricade sealed the fate of the horsemen and their infantry support.

Fauston could see Breka down by the bridge cursing, stomping his foot in anger. His dark eyes found the mage and he pointed at him. The horn blew three times and Fauston knew his moment had come.

The necromancer said, "Come, Ramid. We are summoned."

Fauston walked up to the Baron, ready for his blustering demands. "Give me a shield," the necromancer said simply. A shield was thrust at him. He handed it to Ramid at the same time he accepted his bag of magical apparatus.

The two men walked past the hundreds of eyes that stared down the length of the bridge. Ramid went first, shield held up.

"We only have to get close enough to activate the powder, Ramid. That fire barricade helps as much. Come."

The duo walked slowly, crouching behind their shield. They were half way across the bridge before the Drebhans became concerned and began firing arrows at them.

"A little closer. Closer. Here. We are close enough."

Fauston took several handfuls of the powder and threw it into the wind. The breeze was blowing towards Drebh so the dust quickly found its mark. He intoned the magic words slowly while Ramid waited behind the shield. Arrows thunked into the wood. Fauston was almost finished when a chance missile grazed his shoulder.

"Damn, now I have to start again. Hold that shield straight, Ramid!"

"Yes, master."

More powder, and the charm began again.

"Hurry, master. Soldiers are coming." Ramid was right. Three Drebhans had worked their way around the fire bales and were running towards them, swords in hand.

Fauston finished the last phrases of his spell. Then yelled, "Kill!" in the direction of the running men. A dozen Shanians rose from the bridge deck to trip them, then beat in their brains with mailed fists.

A scream rose from the far side of the river. Corpses rose

from the ground in waves of blood-covered flesh. Men screamed, threw down their weapons and fled. A cheer came from behind the two Riinians. Pounding feet soon followed as the soldiers of Shan charged in force across the river to secure the position now left empty by the fleeing Drebhans. Ramid thought they could have been more thankful as they shoved the two up against the rail. Breka stopped long enough to slap Fauston on the arm, his sore one, now bleeding profusely.

"Well done, magister. Follow me to Lord Grumnor's stronghold. We will soon win the day."

But Fauston made no especial effort to follow the Shanians into Drebh. The two wandered in behind the cheering soldiers, twenty zombies now forming an honor guard around them. The undead did not attack anyone wearing a pouch, so they stumbled about, only attacking when Drebhans came near. The few Shanians who did not wear them fell back, steering as far from the undead line as possible.

A half-hour later Fauston and Ramid found their way through the burning buildings and occasional piles of dead to the headquarters of Lord Grumnor. The dead who littered the ground stayed that way for Fauston would not waste his magics when victory was obviously in hand. A grinning Breka sat inside, his mailed arse on Grumnor's throne. The headless warrior lying beside him was most likely that defunct sovereign. The Baron laughed when he saw Fauston and his servant still clutching the shield.

"I have a surprise for you, *magister.* Look!" He pointed at Bradur who sat at a table eating and drinking. The man had a black eye, marks about his wrists signifying he had recently been bound.

"Seems old Grumnor had him locked away."

Fauston went to the General. "It is good to see you alive, Bradur."

The General tipped his lion headdress in salute. "Just barely. I haven't had a drink in five days." He punctuated this with a guzzle of ale.

"What happened?"

The General worked around a mouthful of bread and cheese. "We were captured coming back from Riin. My squad fought bravely defending our prize but I do not see any of them here now."

"Prize?"

It was Breka who answered that question.

"Yes, would you like to see Bradur's prize?" He stomped a foot on a long box that sat near Grumnor's throne. "The old pirate had no idea what to do with it."

Fauston and Ramid left Bradur to his repast and gathered around the long box. Breka shoved his sword blade between the wood slates and pried. The boards popped off effortlessly, revealing a casket

"A body?" asked Fauston. "Some loved one, Baron?"

"Yes, indeed. But not one of mine."

The large man bent down, pulling a coverlet from the glass-fronted casket. Both Fauston and Ramid gasped when they saw the lovely but pale corpse of Rayahl, Fauston's dead fiancée.

"I got her for a bargain too," laughed Breka. "Only thirty thousand plats."

The necromancer was speechless. It was Ramid who said, "That swine, Frech."

"Swine he might be, but Bradur found him quite reasonable when gold was in the offering."

"Why?" asked Fauston, unable to take his eyes from the visage of his lover.

"Because I need you, *magister.* You proved that today. With your sorcery, my army is unstoppable. I will be king of all the North."

"Worm," hissed the necromancer. "How did you find out—"

Breka's sword came up, pricked Fauston's throbbing throat. "Watch yourself, wizard. You work for me. Until I am finished. Then she is yours. Bradur has been my eyes and ears in Riin. He was sent to find what you valued above all else. So that I might hold it. Until I wished to give it to you. Do we understand each other?"

Fauston's eyes flamed, his teeth gritted but he managed, "Yes, we understand it each other."

"Good," laughed Breka, sheathing his blade. "We hold Drebh. Let's celebrate. Wine! Bring me Grumnor's finest wine!"

And the necromancer drank poor Northern wine as the dying expired around them. Breka would not allow the Drebhans to be slaughtered, raped or pillaged. He wanted the men to fill his ranks, the women to succor these soldiers and the resources of the land to feed his army.

"It is a good day," declared the Baron. "Your zombies did their work well."

Fauston said nothing, but sipped his wine.

"Cheer up, *magister*. We will have a good laugh. Think on it. How is Bradur going to find enough whore necklace for all these men?" The liege-lord punctuated this jest with a rib-shattered slap that sent Fauston's wine cup flying. The wine landed in Ramid's face. The Shanians, even Bradur, laughed.

"We can't go home soon enough, master," hissed Ramid. "Wine stains!"

Even Fauston cracked a grin at this. "Administer to my wound first, Ramid. Then we'll look for some soft water." His grin disappeared as Gorn came in dragging a gray-haired form Fauston recognized, Nilli the crone.

"Look what I found in Grumnor's room?" he said with a snort. He threw the old woman to her knees before Breka.

"So, you conspire against me, Nilli?" asked the Baron while shoving a boot into her belly.

"Mercy, my Baron," the cracked old voice said. "I had no choice."

"Why, old woman?"

"Because of the *Nargesh*. I had to do something. He will bring doom down on us all." She pointed a twisted finger at Fauston.

"What nonsense? This is my pet wizard. He does as I tell him."

Fauston's brow wrinkled at Breka's arrogance but said

nothing.

"*Nargesh,* he is cursed! He uses the black arts from the forbidden book."

At this Fauston blinked. She knew about the *Arcani Diablieri.* Impossible. It was hidden in a secret cubby in his private bedroom. No one went in there, not even Ramid.

"He must be slain, or we will all die."

Breka looked up from the crone at the necromancer. "What do you say to this accusation?"

"Nonsense! She has fallen prey to the rumors, rumors Bradur crushed. I am your servant. There is no curse here. Only dead men that do your bidding."

Breka drew his sword, weighed the old woman's words, then Fauston's. He raised the blade then drove it into the witch's body. She shrieked, gurgled then was quiet.

"Traitorous cow."

He pulled the wide blade out, wiped the blood on the old woman's poor attire. Then pointed it at Fauston.

"Be warned, *magister.* Good work buys you this frozen beauty." He tapped the glass casket. "Poor work, any hint of a curse, and you share Nilli's fate. Understand?"

Fauston nodded grimly. "And Rayahl's casket?"

"I will have it installed in my own headquarters, under a constant guard."

"Good. For I make a promise of my own, Baron Breka. Any harm comes to her and you can worry about more than the babbling of this old witch."

Breka's sword tip came up, poised before Fauston's eyes. The necromancer did not flinch. He spun without haste before he said, "Come, Ramid, I desire my own bed." The servant scurried quickly in behind.

Fauston could hear Breka laugh, throw his sword aside. He called out, "Come, Bradur, I feel like a barrel of ale, three or four of these Drebhan sluts and a hangover in the morning bad enough to split my skull!" The General cheered and joined his master in his jollities. The two Riinians walked away without any further discussion, their twenty undead guardians taking up their position a few steps behind them all the way back to Shan.

Part Three: The Burning Man

"It is not the sweetness of friends but the sharpness of enemies that make a man." – Torinde

BRADUR'S EYES scanned the village just beyond the trees. A soldier behind him dragged his heel and a flashing look of displeasure warned the man to silence.

Something's not right, Bradur thought. There should be more noise. Even if the men were off fighting or hunting or farming, there should be the sound of women sweeping, children playing or old men snoring in their chairs in the sun, something. Not even a dog's bark could be heard over the soft breeze.

No one is here. Have they all fled? Surely if they had known the Shanians were coming they would take their goats and horses, but their chickens, cats and dogs?

Bradur waved his men onto the village road, a rocky patch that led from the fields off to their left to the central well. Fifty men—armed with swords, bows and spears, armored in jerkins of leather with metal plates sewn on with wire stitches—stepped out of the surrounding blackberry canes and into the open.

They waited at their leader's hand gesture. Bows strung, swords out, they advanced toward the silent houses, awaiting treachery.

Maybe someone else has come and killed them or taken slaves? But what slaver would take every dog and cat, donkey and chicken? Plague then, something that kills—everything.

For a second Bradur almost turned his host around and marched back to their camp three miles to the north. Almost. But he didn't see any dead bodies. They'd be flies buzzing in swarms. Nothing like that. There were flies but not anymore than expected. Perhaps fewer, for the horse turds on the road were days hard.

He ran in a crouch to the first house. The door was closed but not locked. He threw the portal open, waving a man with a spear through the doorway. A few seconds later he saw the soldier turn to him, and shrug. No one.

Bradur stepped inside. The table was set. The bed was made in the small single-chambered dwelling. Clean. Nothing out of place. Certainly not the work of slavers or pillagers. The house would be ransacked, the empty walls aflame by torches.

The squad went from house to house but it was the same everywhere. In barns, sheds and corrals. Empty but orderly.

They all left by their own choice. Cleaned up and left. They didn't take anything valuable, as would a rout of fleeing refugees headed for the safety of a castle. Bradur could see this for on the headman's table were dishes of silver. Baskets of bread full, though days dry and uneaten.

A soldier approached bearing an empty cage.

"What is it?" asked Bradur, no longer keeping the silence. The sound of his voice was discordant but welcome.

"They took their birds," the soldier said stupidly.

Or was it so stupid? Not a dog, cat, cow, horse, even so much as a rat had shown up.

"The rabbit hutch around back is empty too."

"They took all the pets, the cattle, everything."

"Yes, sir."

"That doesn't make sense, soldier. People fleeing don't weigh themselves down with birds. And they don't leave the cage!"

"Yes, sir." The soldier looked embarrassed, not sure what to say.

Bradur ignored him. A new thought was forming in his mind. A thought he didn't care for.

"Soldier, find the sergeant. I need to speak to him."

"Yes, sir." The soldier disappeared, to reappear a few seconds later with the man in question, a sturdy fellow named Thorun.

"Sergeant, I want you to spread the men out. Have them look

for anything unusual. Other than the fact there is no one here. Check the ground, the buildings, the trees, anywhere for something – *unexplained*." Bradur gave him a look that asked if he understood his inexact instructions.

"Something unusual. Yes, sir."

"And be careful."

"Yes, sir."

The soldiers collected near the well when the sergeant blew his whistle. A minute then the fifty men were spreading out in pairs.

A half hour passed. Bradur was about to call off this foolish search and return to camp, when Thorun came running.

"Over this way, sir. I think this is what you meant."

Bradur followed the sergeant without comment, down the street, then onto a shady path that cut through the blackberries and ended at a small pond. Five soldiers stood around something that Bradur could not see. Only as he drew up and looked at the wet, loamy soil at the edge of the pond could he make it out. A rectangular indentation as long as a man and almost as wide. His brow wrinkled. What was it? Thorun pointed at another on the far side of the pond, a good twenty feet away. Beyond that was a thick hedge of brambles.

"What do you make of it, sir?" asked the sergeant.

"The only thing I can, Thorun. Magic."

The sergeant's face darkened. Bradur did nothing to banish his worry. "Round up the men. Back to camp immediately."

As Thorun's whistle called the retreat, Bradur took a last look at the two marks. *Footprints*, he thought. What could make such footprints? Then he thought of Fauston the necromancer who waited back in a tent at camp. Well, well, your Worship. I think I've found your sign at last.

FAUSTON WATCHED the smoke rise from the distant hills. People were dying down in the trees by the river. Baron Breka's army was killing those unwilling to join his new kingdom. The necromancer could not hear the screams or smell the blood but he knew they were there all the same. He also knew that the blood was on his conscience.

The first victories in Breka's campaign had been small but decisive. When the Shanians had attacked Drebh the dead had risen to help them. The Drebhian army had fled the field, only to surrender hours later, as the Baron himself took their leader's head.

Bolstered with new troops, Shan had then taken Relh. Only Torn remained, but Fauston agreed with his manservant, Ramid. "*This one feels different*."

"Why do you say that, Ramid?" asked his master.

"I don't know. I suppose it's foolish—" he faltered.

"What? Speak your mind."

"Well, at first we felt like the underdogs, trying to do the impossible. But now—"

"Now the empire seems quite possible—and our master, Baron Breka, less of a barbarous oaf, and capable of –"

"Yes, that is partly it. But—"

"Yes?"

"It's been too easy, master. Something must come to stop us."

"Must it?" Fauston had asked. Ramid had not answered that. And how could he? He just shrugged. But Fauston saw that he too felt this way. Something was coming, and it was coming from Torn.

The necromancer pushed the thought of Ramid and his gloom aside. Instead he studied the river that meandered down to Torn. The farmsteads below were just the outskirts of the second largest town in this area. Only Shan was bigger with its board sidewalks and thirty-seven large structures. A veritable metropolis in this stinking sewer of a wilderness.

Still, I have Rayahl now. Or Breka does.

The year that Fauston had dedicated to Breka's campaign had flown like dust through a sieve. The contract complete, the city-dwellers had thought they'd soon return to Riin and its minarets over-looking sun-gilded shops and theaters. Only Breka had changed the deal. Before it had been money that brought Fauston so many leagues from his perfumed estate and countless slaves. But spies had found out what Fauston wanted the money for—to buy the body of his dead lover, Rayahl, from Frech the Flesh-peddler. A quick exchange of plats and the Baron now possessed that which Fauston desired most.

"Win me this war, corpse-master, and I will give her to you. And as much gold as you deem fair."

What could he do?

Ramid had been crushed when he heard Fauston say, "Yes, of course, my Lord Breka."

Later in private, Ramid spoke his mind. "Master, if I must spend one more month in this rat hole I shall go mad!"

"I give you permission to leave, Ramid. You have been a faithful servant. I will provide you with a letter so good you'll find a new position in the city without delay."

This kindness,—or was it the look of dark defeat in his master's eyes—brought the servant to his knees, begging forgiveness.

And so it went on. More villages, more killing. Always the necromancer calling up the slain to join Breka's ranks, killing until no longer needed. The day's butchery done, Fauston would direct the dead to dig, scoop out their own graves and then retire.

How many? How much longer? Once Torn fell, Breka would rule the four major towns beyond Ghand, the rest, true wilderness where only trolls and nightshades dwelt.

It was almost with a sigh of relief that he heard a new sound. Or lack of sound. Breka's men returned empty-handed, not defeated, not even engaged.

"At last—" he sighed. Something had come to stop him at last.

IF FAUSTON had been a hero in some tale sung by bards in an ale-hall, he'd have got on his milk-white mare and charged down into the valley to save a thousand men with great feats of sorcery. But he was no such thing. Instead he waited for Bradur's messenger to come. This is how it had been all through the previous year. Bradur, ever the general in Breka's new regime, executed Fauston's plans while the sorcerer sat at a table reading dispatches. Breka valued the necromancer far too highly to allow him to be killed by a stray arrow or be captured by the other side.

But will they bother to capture me now? he asked himself. It was the first moment he realized that the Baron of Torn had his own sorcerer. Who might it be? Another necromancer – or someone else?

Fauston went to his tent. Ramid waited there over a boiling pot. He shook his head like a man suffering a dying child.

"What is it, Ramid?" asked Fauston.

"A tragedy, no cumin, no coriander. We will have to make due with these meager wild onions and a handful of dried capers I found in the bottom of a sack."

"Yes, terrible news."

Ramid did not detect the hint of sarcasm in his master's voice. "Yes, yes, how can we do justice to Creamed Trout? And goat meat—"

"Enough! Is it ready to eat?"

The servant looked up at Fauston at last, saw his mood would suffer no foolishness.

"Yes, of course."

"Serve it." Fauston made to walk away.

"What is it, master? Does the battle go badly?"

"Something new. I await a messenger. We must eat quickly."

Ramid asked no more questions. He tore a loaf of day-old bread in half, ladled two bowls and filled his master's wine flagon. The wine inside was now a good southern blend. Breka did not ask his servants to suffer much, despite Ramid's complaints.

The two men ate quickly in silence. Fauston nodded wordlessly his approval of the fish stew. Ramid had enough common sense not to go on about it, but accepted the compliment quietly. It was as he was breaking a second loaf that the messenger arrived. It was Bradur himself. The lanky blond general was covered in Southern-made armor though he retained his lion-skin headdress in place of a helmet.

The swordsman had brought Fauston and Ramid to Shan, a danger-filled journey that had made the rough barbarian a welcome friend in Fauston's camp. The necromancer had complete faith in the general, having seen that he was a good handler of men as well.

"I had to come, your Worship. I didn't think you'd believe what I have to tell from another's lips."

"You have seen it with your own eyes then?" demanded the necromancer.

"Aye, for I could not believe it myself."

"Ramid! Wine for the General!" Fauston waved his guest to a seat by the fire, while standing himself.

In a few short minutes Bradur had described all the strange events in the village to his friend. "It sent more chills down my spine than the ghost tales my grand-dame used to tell by the fire," admitted the tall swordsman. "I won't go back. Nor any of my men."

"Where are your scouts then?"

"Outside the village about a mile, in a copse of firs. The main army joins them on the morrow—Breka will take Torn tomorrow."

"Tomorrow? I haven't enough time to figure this thing out by tomorrow!" The necromancer threw his empty wine cup on the ground.

"Patience, your Worship," said Bradur with a slurp from his own cup. "The siege could last months."

Fauston said nothing more, just looked angrily at the coming daylight beyond the camp.

"Well, I see you're not going to be any fun today," sighed Bradur. "Ramid, come join me at the inn. I'll buy the first round."

The mage's servant looked terrified by the suggestion.

The barbarian laughed. "Forget it. I know your tastes run

towards lovers with downy beards—though I think one of Scarvarde's daughters is a bit on the hairy side."

After Bradur left, his ringing laugh dying away with the wind, Ramid joined his master in a sulk. "Downy beards, indeed! Is it my fault every woman in this country has the face of mule?"

Fauston did not have patience to listen to Ramid once again on the ugliness of northern ladies. A final raised hand told the servant that his master did not wish to be disturbed, as he headed back to bed.

THE NEXT morning, Ramid woke to the sound of marching boots. He pulled his tent flap open, then stood up to see better the Shanian troops that headed for Torn.

"Master, they have begun without us."

Fauston, who sat in a chair beside a smoky morning fire, grunted.

"Master, Baron Breka always brings you down to survey the battlefield, to make sure the charms are in place—"

"*King* Breka grows bold. We are but an insurance policy, to be pulled out once thing things go awry."

"And will they?"

"Undoubtedly. We have no idea what those giant footprints are. Has he recruited an army of stone trolls, or even worse, blood giants? I think we will be called before the lunch hour, so quick-quick, get the breakfast made. I will prepare for—" he paused for a second, lost in a dark thought. " – *battle*."

Preparations were almost a rout activity after the taking of Relh and Drebh, fourteen skirmishes and battles all told. Fauston placed his death charms in the main compartment of his bag, those magics which would raise the dead to fight alongside the soldiers of Breka. The components he brought were but a supplementary supply, for every fighting man in the Baron's war host bore a charm bag filled with the necessary ingredients to keep the zombie forces from attacking them as well as charms to use to resurrect the fallen enemy as well. (This had been partly one of Bradur's innovations. The Blood Guard medals were now attached to the component bag, making it impossible to bear one without the other.)

In the other section of his satchel he placed a silver dagger, a piece of horn taken from a riinocerous, a terrible beast of the Southlands, the ivory now carved with mystic runes, and lastly, his elongating telescope.

"I'm ready, Ramid. Bring my uniform." Fauston said this last with a sneering contempt. The uniform was a suit of leather armor that Breka had insisted he wear whenever on the field of battle. "As if this would protect me from a blast of rune fire or the bite of a shugoron!"

"Wear it to please me, sorcerer," said the Baron. The Lord of Shan's word was law.

After a tough few minutes of wrestling with Ramid, the necromancer was laced in and feeling like a trussed pig. Ramid came back bearing a helmet with metal rivets.

"The helmet, master."

"The helmet be damned!"

"But, master—"

"No, Ramid, I draw the line at this stupid armor. I must see if I am to do my duty, and that bloody thing has a nose guard longer than my entire face. Leave it."

The two men mounted their horses and rode to the side of the line of armed men who filed past, no longer foot soldiers but archers and the occasional mounted knight. Laughter told the necromancer that one of the armed men was Bradur. His lion headdress high on his head, a shield bearing Breka's white hart and his broadsword strapped to his broad back, he bellowed again. "Morning, your Worship. His Royal Majesty has sent me to fetch you. We must inspect the ground for today's victory."

"I thought you said we'd be besieging them for a month."

"Not so – our good friend, Trepsis of Torn has seen to it that is should not happen."

"How so?"

"His army awaits us a mile and a half from here, just across a creek, in the willows."

"But that's madness! He has the advantage, tall sturdy walls and a million arrows."

"Just so, but my scouts report otherwise."

"This smells of sorcery. He wants us to come. He wants to meet us in the open—"

"Also true. His Majesty foresees a swift victory and a completion of his consolidation of the Northlands."

"I need more time. Something is afoot and we have no idea —"

"Old man's nerves."

"You were in that village – tell me you did not feel it."

"Hm, you have a point, but I can not turn Breka's hand. We march on Torn. Come, let us go see the battlefield for ourselves."

"One minute, I need my spyglass."

"But, master, you already—" began Ramid.

"Nonsense, Ramid." Fauston glared at his manservant, then returned to his tent, where he took the black book from under his bed. The volume fit poorly into the bag but Fauston shoved it down then tied the leather straps.

"Alright," he said as he mounted, "Let's begin this fool's escapade."

"IT'S TOO easy," said Fauston for the tenth time. "The ground is level; the creek is of little consequence. Only the willows offer any real cover – and once we are across the stream even these—"

"A quick victory for King Breka and a quick victory for us before we sample all the treasures of Torn." Bradur slapped Ramid on the back, causing the servant to choke on his own spit. "Good luck, sorcerer."

Fauston waved good-bye to the general as he helped his servant to regain his composure.

"That oaf—" began Ramid, his face red as an apple.

"That oaf is heading the charge today. Let us hope he returns to insult us once again."

To this Ramid nodded a grudging acknowledgement.

The horns began to sound along the Shanian lines. Ten thousand men strong , the largest force ever assembled in the Northlands, composed of Shanian knights, Relhian archers and Drebhian lancers. All stood shoulder to shoulder, eying the smaller Tornian army that waited across the stream.

The front line of infantry moved forward until they reached a distance where the first Tornian arrows struck throat and shield. The soldiers stopped and waited for their own archers to come alongside, to release their own rain of death into the ranks that stood before the willows. The Tornians fell before the onslaught but remained on the ground. Later as the Shans came closer, the warriors would scatter Fauston's dust over the dead, their ranks swelling with undead. Until then, they twitched then lie still.

The Torns fell back to the willows as the Shans cheered and poured across the stream. The stragglers gave a weak resistance but most of the Torns disappeared into the trees. Fauston watched this from the back of the Shan ranks with his spyglass. "Too easy," he said for the eleventh time.

The cheers of the Shans were cut short as the willows separated like blades of grass. Something large was rising up from the shadows to stand taller than the tallest tree. Fauston dropped his spyglass for he could not make out the vast shape of the thing through the lens.

"At last—" he sighed, like man awaiting a verdict at trial. "—here it comes."

The shape was man-like though having no features of face except a vast mouth. This orifice opened in a scream even the distant sorcerer could hear. The roar was followed by a massive swing of a fist as the giant thing stepped from the forest and into the ranks of the surprised Shans. The fists, each as large as a carriage, slammed down onto screaming men, swept left and right, knocking down everything in its path, only to be trampled by its massive feet.

Fauston drove the panic from his mind. He pulled the riinocerous horn from his bag and blew into the instrument, watching its many glyphs and runes glow with power. The device allowed the necromancer to control the legions of dead from the safety of his perch.

He smiled to see the first of the dead rising up from the creek bed, stumbling toward the giant. Minute shambling forms moved on the enemy, only to be flattened like so many ants. The vast feet crushed zombies and knight into red ruin, bodies too mangled for the necromancer's magic to animate them.

Fauston brought his spyglass up. He looked more carefully at his adversary. What was it? How could he fight something he knew nothing about? He'd have to get closer.

"Come, Ramid," he bellowed over the din of steel and violence. "We have to get close enough to see this thing better."

"I can see it just fine from here – it's so big."

Fauston ignored his servant's grumblings and started toward the front.

After ten minutes walking, Ramid shouted, "Look, master, Bradur's charging."

The general and his knights came from the flank, running over any Torns who remained on the field. The lances of the cavalry were not meant for these few resistors but for the giant. The arrowhead of the charge came toward the towering figure, aiming for the legs, but at the last second the horses shied and floundered, many dislodging their riders.

Fauston watched the following disaster through his glass, but it was not the dying knights or their panicked horses that drew his attention. It was something he had not even guessed might happen. Fauston watched as the gigantic man shape swung its fist at a horse, the fist-like bulge on the end connecting with a brutal, rib-smashing blow. What came away from that swing was not the same fist but a larger one, the horse now part of the colossus. Stomping feet also came away larger, encrusted by the contact.

"It grows, master," Ramid whispered next to Fauston's ear.

"Closer, Ramid. We've got to get where I can see this thing in detail."

Moving towards the creek became difficult now as infantry and knight fled before the crushing blows of the giant. Bradur, who had survived the first charge with horse still under him, pulled back to throw his lance spear-style at the large legs. A few others did likewise, then fell back, attempting to hold the ranks from utter panic. An orderly retreat saved many lives as the archers moved up, feathering the colossus with diminutive missiles.

Finally Fauston reached the last rank of archers. His glass could now make out the closest details of the giant that stomped and bellowed at the rain of arrows. The newcomer's eye could make out a wicker structure, cages in which screamed and moved many living things. It is a giant man made of living flesh, he realized. And worst of all, the entire structure appeared to be burning, not with a black charring fire but a weird, blue wizard flame.

"This is dark magic," he said to himself. "I have seen this before. In the *Arcani Diablieri*."

Dropping his bag, Fauston opened the flap to retrieve the black volume. Ramid's eyes grew wider as he saw what his master held.

"Master, no, tell me it isn't—"

Fauston said nothing. He was too busy flipping through pages covered in obscene diagrams and terrible script in a search for a certain dark secret. He stopped at last. "'The Burning Man'," he said to Ramid as much as to himself. "I know of this thing. I must read this now to see how we might destroy it. Ramid, keep people away as much as you can, while I –"

With that the necromancer read for several minutes. At last he looked up, white-faced, his eyes wide.

"What is it, master?"

"Life magic, Ramid. My enemy uses living things against me. The counter spell is difficult but it is terrible to wield."

"No, master, burn the book and let us flee this madness."

"No, find a sword, quickly, and a dying man."

Ramid stumbled away, not sure what to do. His training told

him to do as his master bid, but his brain burned with the knowledge that they were committing the greatest of evils.

"Over here, master," called the servant at last. "This man is yet alive – for now."

Fauston ran over to the soldier. The giant had crushed his right arm, his bare ribs bleeding. He would expire in minutes, to rise again as an undead warrior.

"Good knight," Fauston addressed him seeing he was one of Bradur's riders. "How would you like to avoid the necromancy? To die here a clean death?"

The man nodded yes, blood dripping from his chin.

"Then prepare yourself," was all Fauston said. He picked up the man's own sword, a good blade forged by southern hands. The necromancer read a few words from the black book, applied some of the man's blood , then buried the blade deep in his throat. The knight gasped once and expired.

"No master, it is too terrible."

"You have no idea—"

Bradur rode up behind the wizard. "There you are. I've been looking for you everywhere. You're not supposed to be this close."

"I had to. I needed to see."

"And what sorcerer's trick can you offer? My men are dying out there."

"This blade – it is the answer, but—"

"Think nothing of it!" said Bradur grabbing the blade before Fauston could stop him.

"No!"

"Yes, but how does it work?" Bradur looked at the blade, noticing the weird fire that danced along the edge, the same blue flame that covered the giant.

"The blade will kill that thing—"

"Good, let's test it." Bradur made to ride away.

"Wait, Bradur, once the thing appears to be dying, throw away the sword. Do not press the attack."

The barbarian general made no promise, only cried out, "My

men are dying!" then rode straight for the creek bed.

"Come, Ramid. We must follow."

"Master, it is forbidden."

"We have to – for Bradur's sake."

Ramid made no reply but picked up Fauston's bag, and followed.

Fauston abandoned trying to see what was going on through his spyglass. Instead he ran toward the giant and the rapidly advancing horseman. Bradur flew like an arrow towards the towering shape that cast its long shadow over the battlefield.

The giant no longer stomped the undead who collected about it but spun its eyeless face for more living victims. The battlefield no longer held any foes, all the foot soldiers had fallen back behind the ranks of archers. These men stopped firing as Bradur charged across the empty field toward the colossus.

The monster roared its challenge and lurched toward the advancing knight. The Burning Man's huge legs ate up yards with each step and soon the two combatants met. The giant swung its terrible fist at Bradur, who ducked the blow, then swung his own puny weapon. The result was instantaneous. The blade passed through wicker and flesh, pulling away the blue fire and dissolving the fingers that came away as black ash.

The titan screamed and swung again. But the sword cut again and chunks fell off the other fist. Riding in behind the giant, Bradur scored another swipe that landed on the leg, making it buckle.

Disaster struck then for the lone attacker. The colossus lost its balance and fell backwards onto the rider and mount. The charger screamed, dying in a tangle of living, blue-burning flesh.

Fauston and Ramid ran over the empty battlefield, dodging bodies and other small obstacles. They could see the giant try to stand, howl in its rage then fall back. A black sickness grew over its body of caged flesh. Ramid could see the trapped men and women, dogs, cats, horses and birds that made up the living captors of the giant's limbs. All those villagers, sacrificed to make this evil engine of death, he realized. An entire village. Faces crumbled to ashes as the blue flame was pulled from the cages, the titan's arms and legs collapsing into black, fetid ash.

Fauston swore when he saw Bradur's head pop out of one pile, the blade following, cutting more and more of the gigantic body away.

"Bradur! Throw the blade away!" screamed the necromancer. His servant soon joined him, calling to the general.

But Bradur did no such thing. He hacked and howled until all the arms and legs were but a black ruin. Only the great body remained.

"Bradur, throw it—"

Fauston never finished the sentence. The general raised the blade for the killing blow into the head, stabbed then was thrown back in a blast of blue fire that took his body twenty feet across the riverbank.

"Quickly, Ramid, we must—"

The servant was ahead of his master, already running across the stones to the far side of the creek. Fauston would have joined him but laughter tore him from his urgency.

The head of the monster, all its body had crumbled into ash, every caged beast, man and child, consumed by terrible magic. But standing in the pile of soot was still one man-sized form. Fauston looked at the blackened shape and recognized it, like a distance memory.

More laughter followed a finger pointing at the necromancer. "Finally," it croaked. "Finally, you have taken the dark path."

Fauston stepped closer, staring at the charred face. Could it be?

"Kesush?—"

More laughing. The old bookseller's features smiled despite being composed of burnt ash. "Yes, it is I, Kesush."

"But why? Did Torn pay you so well?"

"Fool! I came to Torn, not they to me. You needed a push. I gave you one."

"No! I will never use that book again."

"Stupid—" Kesush's shape was beginning to crumble. "You have taken it from me—willingly. You now bear the curse. And I – I go to sweet oblivion." With a last laugh, the body of Kesush, the first to be laid inside the Burning Man, followed the others.

"No! Ramid, help me—"

The manservant could not hear his master, for he was across the stream, standing over Bradur's broken form. The general still lived, but the shards of the sword blade were buried deep in his chest. The lion headdress was gone and his hair flowed around him like a golden crown.

"Ramid—" he gasped through strained and bloodstained teeth. "The pouch – quickly."

Ramid looked at the small pouch around Bradur's throat, the charm that would resurrect him on death. Ramid pulled it off and threw it away.

"It's no good, Bradur," Ramid said through wet tears. "There is too much death powder in the air. You will still rise—"

"Not that pouch. On my left side, on my belt."

Ramid dug through black cloth to find a large bulging pouch on the General's belt. He tore through the sacking, retrieved an earthenware cylinder, sealed with black wax.

"Yes, Bradur, I have it. What is it?"

"King's Fire. I got it in the Southlands, to show Breka."

King's Fire, the king of Riin had a dozen siege catapults that threw the deadly liquid canisters into the enemy's midst. Upon contact with the air, the liquid instantly burst into a dark orange flame.

"What do you want—?"

"Cover me with it. Give me a hero's death. Save me from the necromancer."

"I – I—" stammered Ramid.

"I never could stand all these stinking zombies."

The manservant smiled weakly, remembering Bradur's first experience with Fauston's undead.

He raised the bottle as Fauston ran up, "No, Ramid, don't! I can —-"

Ramid's arm came down, the canister opened over dying man. Both servant and master recoiled from the sudden burst of orange fire. Bradur gave one last cry of joyful abandon as his life was extinguished in a spasm of heat and destruction.

"No! No! I could save him. I could save him," moaned Fauston as he watched the general's body reduced to charred bones.

"Ramid! I will have your head for this. Ramid!"

The servant did not hear his master. He walked away, looking for something. There it was! The lion headdress. He picked it up, brushing the dust from the fur.

"Ramid! Come back here!"

Ramid put the headdress on. It smelled of sweat and blood and worse. He laughed, and just kept walking. ✸

Made in the USA
Lexington, KY
05 March 2013